ROUNDFIRE LEGENDS
&
CREATESPACE

THE
HASTINGS
WATCHMAN

CHRONICLES OF THE VANCITY VIGILANTE

WRITTEN BY
GREGORY PATRICK TRAVERS

© roundfirelegends.net

Story One: the Hooded Killer........5

Story Two: Rise of the Hipster......49

A man lizard emerges from the shores of English Bay. It is up to Jake and the Watchman to subdue this murderous villain before it's too late.

Jake takes on the role of the Watchman to stop The Freak once and for all. But enemies old and new seem to be popping up everywhere. If he wants to save the city, he's going to have to give it all he's got!

This one is for Vancouver...

Story One: the Hooded Killer

I've been a reporter for the Vancouver Sun for about three years now. I suppose I should be thankful that I have such a secure job doing what I love but I must say that in the last little bit I have become bored with it all. There hasn't been a story that I've covered in a while that was more fun that it was work. Maybe I've just started to settle in and like a marriage; the flame that once burned at the beginning has dimmed throughout the years of predictable repetition. Sometimes I wonder if I'll ever feel that same excitement I felt when I was hunting my first story…The mystery of the Hastings Watchman.

I was younger then, the budding age of 23, trying to find myself in an unforgiving, forever revealing world. The dreams of being a rock star were starting to seem more and more ridiculous and the things that I used to get away with on account of my boyish good looks were catching up to me now that the years of smoking and poor diet were starting to take their toll. It was a time where I needed to find something of my own, something I could say that I *was*, something honest and true…something that would make the girls want to fuck me.

I decided that I wanted to be a journalist and tackle the real stories being left out of these cookie-cutter media establishments who gossiped more than they informed. But sadly, with no schooling or experience my resumes found themselves huddled in the trash with apple cores and Styrofoam coffee cups. I couldn't get an interview anywhere.

One night, sitting over a beer at the Hastings Warehouse I heard one of the off-duty cooks talking to a waitress about how he had heard there were homeless people going missing around the Lower East Side. Apparently the VPD had picked up a few bodies in the last few weeks lying dead on the pavement in the middle of the street.

"Maybe they just overdosed," said the waitress, twirling her hair and chewing her gum. I wondered why, for a girl who could obviously multi-task very well, my burger was taking so fucking long.

"No, they all died the same way," said the cook, trying his best to keep his eyes from sinking chest ward. "They all got their throats slit."

"Ew. That's gross," she said. And she walked off, leaving the kid back to his beer and leaving me with a brilliant idea. You see, as far as I knew, no one had broken this story in the media yet. If I could get the scoop on who was killing these homeless people then maybe a job wouldn't be so hard to get anymore.

The first person I hit up was Johnny from the Cambie, another one of the restaurants in that little block on the Lower East Side. He wasn't a server or a cook, he just stood outside and sold weed. Ask anyone who knew him though; they'd say he was just as important to that place as any beer or burger. He also happened to be my personal weed dealer so if I was going to get an honest and informed opinion about these so-called murders, Johnny was the guy.

"What'll it be?" he asked, puffing on his cigarette, his hands stuffed inside his sweater pockets.

"Actually, I came here to ask you something."

"Well, I'm not the Customer Service desk at the mall, so if you want to talk I'd suggest you buy something."

I groaned. "Fine, fuck it," I said, reaching into my pocket and pulling out a crumpled twenty bill. He took the cash and slipped me a baggy with the other hand.

He smiled, "Okay, what's on your mind?"

"What do you know about these homeless people getting murdered the last few weeks?"

"Not much. I saw the road blocked off a couple days ago and someone laying there. That's about it. I don't really follow the life and times of crack heads. Why don't you go ask Nancy?" He pointed across the street to a feeble old lady panhandling on the corner.

"That's what I paid twenty bucks for?" I said.

"No, you paid twenty bucks for weed and I gave you the information out of the goodness of my heart, ya goof. Fucking smart ass…"

I jogged across the street to Nancy. "Excuse me," I said, "I was wondering if I could have a few words with you. My name is Jake Dunlop…I'm a reporter."

She looked me up and down, "You don't look like a reporter."

"I didn't realize that reporters had a look." I replied.

She lifted her crinkled Starbucks cup to my face and jingled the change around, "As long as they have pockets."

I rolled my eyes as I reached back into my pocket for more change. I was getting robbed today.

After I dropped a couple toonies in the cup she smiled a toothless smile and provided some answers to what had been going on. "The cops won't go public, but it's a serial killer. How could it not be, right? They all died the same way; Throat slit, out in the street…Terrible. I knew all of them, you know, the ones who died. We all stay at the shelter when we can. They were all good people. They think just because we're poor our lives doesn't have value. They won't find whoever did it, they won't even try. It's just another bum dead. Thank god for the Watchman."

My head poked up from the pad I was taking notes on, "The Watchman? Who's that?"

"No one knows," she said. "He appears every now and then when one of us is in trouble. Like a guardian angel. He'll find who's doing this. He'll get them."

"Uh, thanks," I said, putting my notepad back in my pocket. "Sorry, what shelter were the victims staying at?"

"The Thompson House on East Hastings. We all stay there."

Thanks, Nancy." I said. "Take care of yourself."

"My name's Marie."

"Oh. Sorry. Thanks, Marie." I walked back across the street. "Her name's not even Nancy," I said to Johnny as I passed.

"Like I know what her name is..." I heard him say
behind me.

* * * * * * * * * * * * * * * * * *

I decided that I would stakeout the shelter where
Marie said the victims had stayed in the past.
Maybe then I would catch something. That night I
ate dinner in my apartment and, after doing the
dishes and taking a shower, I dressed up in my
darkest jeans and a black hoodie, grabbed my
camera and headed off into the night.

The place wasn't hard to find, it was one of the
only buildings that didn't have a big AXEL
INDUSTRIES sign boarded up. You see, much of East
Hastings had been under construction during the
last little bit in an attempt to clean up the area and
make it more inviting to Vancouverites. This was
great news to the middle to high class folks who
went out of their way to avoid the area they saw as
scummy and drug ridden, but in order to make
room for these new condos and coffee shops they
had to tear down a few of the low-income housing
buildings and thus, inadvertently making the
homeless problem even bigger. In the midst of the
construction, the three storied shelter stood alone.

During the day you would find many of the
shelter's inhabitants congregated outside, smoking

cigarettes and scheming plans to make a buck for the day, but after 11 o clock, curfew, the street that used to come alive, like some sort of crackhead mardi gras, was now deserted.

At around midnight it started raining pretty hard. Living in Vancouver you come to expect large amounts of rain, but still, it pissed me off. I was thinking of calling it a night and heading back home to my warm bed...but then something happened. It was something I couldn't believe and something that even to this day I doubt if it really happened like I thought it did. But here it is...

As I pulled my hoodie over my head as a makeshift umbrella my eyes were pulled across the street to where an old, raggedy homeless man ran against the pelting precipitation towards the front steps of the shelter. At first I thought he was just trying to get out of the rain. But it wasn't that. He was being *chased*. Behind him, a dark, bulky figure was pouncing down on him like a dog. The hooded attacker pounced on the old man and tackled him to the wet concrete.

With some embarrassment, I must admit, my first reaction was one of excitement and not one of concern for the old man. How lucky was I that my stakeout would give me front row seats to one of the homeless killer's attacks. This was the story I was looking for!

I tried to make out more details of the attacker but between the distance, his hidden face and the rain, it was a near impossibility. As the two of them struggled on the ground another figure fell from above and landed gracefully on his feet not four feet away from them. His face, like the attackers, was also covered. But instead of a hoodie he wore a wool toque and a black bandana over his face. He also wore a leather jacket that had little spikes on the shoulders like the punk rockers I would see outside Funky Winker Beans. The leather shimmered as the rain bounced off it, reflecting the moonlight. There was something strong and proud about this mysterious man. I knew immediately that he had come to stop the attack. So did the Hooded Killer.

The attacker leaped from his prey and darted towards the man in the leather jacket. He jabbed at the man with a large knife but the jabs were dodged with ease. I had never seen someone move so fast in my entire life. Then the man in the leather jacket returned with a Bruce Lee roundhouse kick that connected directly with the Hooded Killer's jaw and sent him stumbling backwards.

This was too good of a photo-op to miss. I pulled out my camera and set up to snap a photo. Once my flash went off my position would be spotted, I only had one shot. Back and forth they went at it; the man in the leather jacket seemed to thwart the knife-wielding attacker's advances effortlessly. He dipped low to the ground and came in with a sweep kick that dropped the Hooded Killer hard to the ground. Seizing my moment, I snapped the photo. The flash lit up the street like lightning.

The man in the leather jacket spun towards me, taking his attention off his foe just for a moment, but a moment was all it took for the Hooded Killer to jump to his feet and drive his blade into the man in the leather jacket's side. He dropped to the floor beside the homeless man and the Hooded Killer ran off into the darkness.

I stood in shock for a moment, unsure if I should run for my life or go help the two men who lay bleeding on the concrete. Before I could make up my mind I watched in utter amazement as the man in the leather jacket rose up to his feet, hopped a nearby fence and was gone.

Marie was right. Not only was there someone out there stalking Vancouver's homeless but there was also someone out there stalking the stalkers...The Hastings Watchman. I could have sworn that part was the crack pipe talking.

This was the story of the year! I rushed home in a hurry to get into some dry clothes and my bed.

After all, I needed my rest to be fresh for the next morning. There were three major papers in Vancouver and thanks to the Hooded Killer and the Watchman I was *sure* I was about to be employed at one of them.

****

"He's like some sort of ninja...but more than a ninja. Like...Like a guardian angel in a leather jacket. I swear to god, I watched him get *stabbed* and then get up and hop a fence like it was nothing. He fell out of thin air"

Paul Dennis, the silver-haired editor of the Vancouver Sun, sat back in his seat, adjusted his tie and looked me over, "That's quite a story," he said. "I just have one question..."

"Sure," I said, smiling.

"Who are you and how the hell did you get passed my secretary?"

"Well, that's two questions, sir," I answered. "But I would be happy to answer them both. My name is Jake Dunlop, I'm a reporter. And that being said, as a reporter, I am naturally a pretty sneaky guy. I get into places where few can."

"Is that supposed to impress me? That you snuck into my office?"

I knew he was asking me that rhetorically, but I really *did* think it would impress him.

He handed the papers and the photo back, "I appreciate the offer, kid. But please get out of my office before I call security."

"But sir, there's a killer on the loose!"

He slammed his fist on his desk, "Says you! I've been doing this for twenty years and you think you're just going to waltz in here off the street, talking about super heroes and tell me how to do my job? These bums kill each other all the time. Over *drugs*. It's nothing special. Now get the fuck out of my building!"

Sensing it was time to leave; I took my files and walked out of the office closing the door on his last profanities. As I turned to leave I bumped into his secretary, a super fox in a black dress that I snuck by on the way in. I smiled at her, she smiled back.

"Hey," I said. "I'm Jake Dunlop. I'm a reporter."

"I'm Diana," she said, extending her hand. Her hands were soft, her eyes were brown. I basically was in love. When I came out of my trance, it

looked like she had been waiting for me to say
something. Then she repeated herself, "Mr.
Dennis? How do you know him?"

"Oh, yeah," I said. "Good guy, that guy. We're like
brothers, me and ol' Pauly. Love that guy."
She laughed a little, I didn't say anything. It was
kind of awkward for a little second and then I just
said, "Diana, I want to take you out for dinner."

She stared at me for a second, sizing me up. I could
tell she was weighing my, what she perceived as,
sense of power and connections verses my pudgy
love handles, cheap haircut and a pubic hairy
beard. I didn't mind; hot girls are like that...and she
was super crazy hot. Plus, she worked for one of
the biggest papers of the city. She obviously was
very particular about who she lets take her out. But
hey, sometimes you win and sometimes you lose.
This time, for some reason unannounced to me, I
won. She gave me her number.

Walking out of the building onto Robson, I stood
amongst the afternoon traffic and just laughed for
a bit. I couldn't believe she agreed to go out with
me; girls are so gullible. I had been in a major
slump recently so it was nice to be getting a little
love...even if it was based on complete bullshit.

I headed on to the Province building to continue
my search for a job. I walked with my head high,

glowing with the confidence of a man who had just successfully tackled the female species. I stood outside the building and flipped through a copy of the Province looking to find the name of the Editor. I found his name and headed inside.

I went straight to the security desk and smiled at the stone-faced Somalian guard. "Hello, I'm Jake Dunlop. I'm a reporter...For the Sun. I'm here to see Donald."

I went with the reporter for the Sun bit because I figured the competition would love to steal a story from a freelancer and I only said the editor's first name because it makes it sound like we knew each other personally.

The guard gave me a look over and picked up the phone. After a moment he put it down and nodded me towards the elevator. "Floor 28," he said.

I tipped my imaginary hat and was on my way. Easy. Peasy.

While I was on my way up in the elevator I stared at the picture I had taken the night before. It was really good. I was impressed with myself. I took it just as the Hooded Killer hit the floor from that sweep kick. The Watchman stood over him in the rain looking all badass and cool. Hard to believe that only seconds after the picture was snapped the Watchman was bleeding on the floor and the killer had got away...I guess I was sort of to blame for that... But it *was* a really good picture though.

* * * * * * * * * * * * * *

Donald Bekinshier, the editor of the Province, sat behind his desk staring down at the photo after I had told him all that I had witnessed. He hadn't kicked me out of his office yet, which was more than I could say about grumpy, old Mr. Dennis at the Sun. I accredited it to his youth.

He shifted in his seat and rubbed his chin. "I like what you got here, Mr.–?"

"Dunlop. Jake Dunlop."

"Of course," he said. "I like what you have here, Jake. This could be a big story. I'll give you three hundred dollars for the pic. What do you say?"

 "I was kind of looking for a chance to be a reporter," I admitted.

He looked down at his lap for a moment and then said, "Gee, I wish it worked like that Mr. Dunlop. The fact is we have staff writers who went through a lot to get here. We have enough competition in-house, never mind the random turncoats from the

Sun. But we do pay handsomely for leads and...pictures like these."

He kept smiling at me. I think he was trying to act "buddy, buddy" but it came off really, "weirdy, creepy"

Three hundred dollars wasn't too bad for a picture. I was eager for cash on the account of the recent date I made with Diana from the Sun so I took the money. I did feel a little bit slimy about handing off this story so easily but the thought of getting Diana naked after I blew her mind with an ass kicking expensive dinner alleviated most of my guilt. Mr. Bekinshier handed me an envelope filled with twenties, shook my hand, and sent me back into the streets; down a picture of the Watchman and up a cheque for three hundred dollars.

That night I made reservations at Le Crocodile, one of the fanciest French restaurants in the city. I had never had French food before, but hey, it looked sexy and it was expensive. *Fuck it*, I thought. I had to set the mood if I was going to nail Diana. It had been a long time since life went so well for me. *Maybe,* I thought. *Things are going to start changing for me around here.*

****

I rolled out of bed at 10am, already excited about my date with Diana. I walked to the kitchen with a hop in my step and ballroom music playing in my head. I laughed as I poured myself a cup of instant coffee and a bowl of Lucky Charms. "More like *get Lucky*, Charms!" I said as a dropped in my spoon and headed to the television room. I sat down on the couch, put my feet up on the coffee table and turned on the television to see the morning news.

I almost dropped my coffee when I saw the picture I had just sold Donald Bekinshier right there on the screen. But the title read, "Bandanna Killer Hunts Homeless."– Which was, if you've been paying *any* attention at all, the complete opposite of how it went down. Bekinshier completely twisted my story to make the Watchman the bad guy. I immediately regretted handing over the story to him. I was so blindsided by the three hundred dollars and Diana's vagina that I just took the money and ran.

Audrey Mason, the morning anchorwoman, was already in mid conversation with the field reporter on the split screen…

"That's right, Audrey," he said, standing outside the Thompson House. "Already six homeless individuals have been killed over the last three weeks. The Chief of the VPD has refused to comment on an ongoing investigation but many witnesses report seeing the people in question lying in the street in *pools of blood*.

"That must have been very disturbing." she said from her desk.

"A very disturbing sight indeed, Audrey," agreed the field reporter.

My picture of the Watchman and the Hooded Killer came back on the screen. Audrey Mason continued, "Now this picture here is taken from today's front page of the Province. It shows the man who is believed to be behind these attacks, a man called the "Hastings Watchman" by the Lower East Side residents. Covered face, a toque and a black bandana. Have the police any word on if the murders are gang related?"

"No word yet on any possible gang relations," said the field reporter. "As of right now, not much is known about the suspect. The police are keeping very close lipped at this time."

"Has anyone mentioned any possible terrorist ties or agenda this sadistic murderer and self-proclaimed "Watchman" might have?"

"That's a very good question, Audrey. With the face covered like it is, it's hard to tell if he is indeed a Muslim—"

I shut the TV off and whipped my remote down on the couch. How could they just make up news like that? How could they just *lie* to millions of people? I had to see the article for myself so I headed over to the BLENZ by my house and grabbed the nearest copy of the Province I could find. The headline read, "HASTINGS KILLER ON THE LOOSE!" With the picture I took directly below it.

 I have to be honest with you, when I saw the words, "Photo taken by Jake Dunlop." written in small font at the bottom corner of the picture, I stopped being angry. *Look on the Brightside*, I thought. I took a photo that was on the front page of a newspaper read by *millions* of people. Now *that* was a conversation starter I could use at dinner with Diana!

 Maybe the story was a lie and sure, I didn't get an actual job out of it, but with this thing on my resume I wasn't too far off from seeing that happen. They fingered the wrong guy but so what? It's not like I knew him or anything. What was he doing around fighting people like that anyway? Besides, no one knew who he was. He could just stop going out dressed like that and never have to worry. Everybody wins.

But no matter what I told myself, the guilt of what I had done sat dormant and slowly ate at me. I tried to force it out of my head as I got ready for dinner. After ironing my shirt I gave Diana a ring to confirm the date.

"Le Crocodile! How nice," she said over the phone.

"Reservation is for seven thirty. Shall I pick you up for seven?"

"Well, you know what? I think I'm going to have to meet you there. I'm just out and about doing some things, no point in dropping off the car."

"Okay, sounds good. So...La Crocodile at seven thirty." My voice went up in pitch. It did that when I talked to pretty women. I hated it.

"Can't wait," she said.

****

I sat at our table at the Crocodile snacking on bread rolls and sipping on a glass of wine poured from the bottle of Cabernet Sauvignon I had ordered us. It wasn't until about seven forty five before I noticed Diana was late, I was looking at the menu and I got distracted. Really nice restaurants always have these really small dishes. Like one prawn on a rice cake over a small pool of sauce or something like that. I found it ridiculous what people found to be "classy." I would have been just as content with a twenty-piece chicken nugget meal from McDonalds. But hey, the bitches love fancy restaurants, right?

At around ten to eight my phone rang. It was Diana.

I answered, "Hello?"

Her voice spoke on the other end, "Hello, *Jake*. Enjoying Le Crocodile?"

"Just waiting for you to get here," I said, sipping the Sauvignon.

Her tone quickly changed, "Well *I'm* not coming, so you're going to be waiting a while."

I nearly choked on my bread role. "Excuse me?"

"Mr. Jake Dunlop, *I'm a reporter*....You're so full of shit. I know you snuck passed me to get into my dad's office! I know you're not a reporter! You think you're smooth? You think I'm gullible or something?"

"Are you crazy? Gullible? Pssh! As if...Wait a second, did you say *dad*? Mr. Dennis is your—"

"My *father*," she said to my embarrassment. "He told me all about you and you two definitely aren't the brothers you said you were. God, you're all the same. Don't call me anymore."

"Wait...So you knew all this when I called you before? Why didn't you just tell me off then and save me the trip?"

"Liars get lied to," she said. "I know your sleazy, little boy type. I know you don't give a fuck about French restaurants and the only reason you made a reservation there is because you thought I would be so impressed at your culture I'd throw my panties to the wind. I know you'd much rather be at McDonalds eating a big mac."

"Chicken nuggets, actually. But so what? How do you know I just won't up and leave to go hit up drive thru?"

She paused on the other end of the phone and then said, "Because you probably got all dressed up, looking all nice. You probably ordered a bottle of wine already because you're not enough of a gentlemen to wait for me, and you don't want to get up and leave because all the fancy rich people might laugh at you and that just kills you because you're a little boy. So what you're going to do is sit there and eat dinner alone like a bitch, just so it looks like that's what you meant to do. Because you're a *big man*. Congratulations on selling your picture to the enemy. Hope the money is well spent."

"Diana, I—"

"Don't bother," she said. Then she hung up.

I picked up my wine glass and took a sip. Man, she really took me for a ride, making me come all the way to the restaurant and wait for her like a dummy. I have to say...it made me want her even more. Who was I kidding, she was right. I wasn't about to get up and do the walk of shame through the restaurant. Plus, I already ordered a bottle of wine and some bread rolls.

So I stayed and ate my dinner.

****

I left Le Crocodile still shaking my head with a smile. That Diana was really something, playing me like that, leaving me to wait for her even though she knew full well that she wasn't going to come. At least I got to see what it's like at a fancy restaurant, finally. Meh, nothing special; too many forks, the waiter took himself way too serious, the duck l'orange I had was good...but definitely not worth the sixty bucks I paid for it. For sixty bucks that duck better suck me off and tickle my balls.

I stood by my car, fiddling with my keys. The bottle of wine I downed was starting to work its familiar magic. A few moments later I was in the car, feeling stuffed, buzzed and ready to go home to jerk away my worries to some good old internet porn. As I pulled out of parking and turned onto the road, I looked into my rear-view checking for cops. Like I said, I was buzzed. That's when I saw someone looking back at me from the back seat.

I stomped on the breaks and yelled, "Holy shit!"

I quickly reached for the door but was restrained by an arm in a leather jacket. The man put a knife to my throat and I froze in my seat. I looked back into the rear-view and this time I got a good look at his face. I couldn't believe it—it was the Watchman! The same bandanna covering his face, the same wool toque pulled low on his head. Underneath his guise his skin was cracked and scarred. His eyes looked into mine. "Keep driving," he said. His voice was low and crackly like someone who had been smoking for years.

I did what he said. I was too scared to say anything back. The ride was silent as we went on, with only a "Left here" and a "Right here" coming from beneath his bandana. We found ourselves parked across the street from the Thompson House.

I finally got the courage to say something. "You're not going to kill me, are you?"

"If I wanted you dead, you'd be dead." he said plainly.

"I see...So...We're just hanging out?"

"Shut up," he replied. "You put me in a bad spot, Jake. I've been on this guy's tail since the murders began almost two months ago. Then you come along with your camera and fuck everything up. Cops are all over this city looking for me now. I'm not safe anywhere."

"I know, I know...I feel really bad about the whole thing. I never meant it to be like that. I didn't know they were going to pin the murders on you."

"The man you sold the pictures to...Donald Bekinshier—"

"From the Province?"

"Yes."

"What about him?"

"He does business with the one behind the killings. The story against me was his way of throwing off the police. The real man behind the murders is Axel Benjamin"

"Axel Benjamin? The construction guy? Are you sure? Why?"

Axel Benjamin was the CEO of Axel Industries; one of the richest people in Vancouver. It was his company that got the contract to re-do the Lower East Side. It didn't make sense that on his free nights he went around killing homeless people.

"The Thompson House refused to sell the land," said the Watchman. "It's been owned by the church for years. He's sent in henchman to try to muscle them out…They refused. This is his next move."

"So he's just going to kill all the homeless people? That's a lot of people."

"He won't have to. The people in the shelter are scared, some have already hopped trains out of town and others are ready to follow. And now that the story has been on the news it won't be long before the public starts to become afraid…And they'll point the figure at us: The low-lifes. The good-for-nothings. They'll make the church sell the property."

"That sounds kind of far-fetched," I said, despite my inner-voice urging me not to upset the man with a knife to my neck.

He took the knife away and reached inside his leather jacket, pulling out a photo and handing it to me. There was a man, a large man, standing over a counter, talking to what looked to be a clerk of some sort. What stood out the most was the man's jaw. It was red and swollen, really ugly looking.

"That's Jeremy Stands," said the Watchman. "I took the picture when he came into the shelter the other day. I had been hanging around there, trying to learn some information. Do you see his jaw?"

"Yeah, it's fucked." I said. "What happened?"

"I kicked him in the face the night you took that photo. I wear steel toe boots. That kick would have knocked most people out...Stands is built tough."

I sat back in my seat, "That's the guy?! The guy in the hood? The killer?"

"That's him. He's Axel's bodyguard and head grease ball. These are bad people, Jake. This story needs to be told."

I took out a cigarette and lit it up. It was hard to believe all this stuff and yet, not that hard at all. It was all very Scooby-Doo. "So how are we supposed to catch this guy in the act?"

"That's your part," he answered.

"Me?"

"Of course," he said. "You're Jake Dunlop...You're a reporter." And then, though I couldn't tell for sure because of the bandana on his face, I swore he smiled at me. "If you're interested, meet me here tomorrow night at ten...I'll find you."

Then he opened the backseat door and ran off into the alley, out of my sight.

****

I woke up the next day and turned on my TV to the morning news. Audrey Mason sat at her desk in the midst of a story, "...Scientists who have been testing the radioactivity in the water have warned that since the meltdown of the nuclear power plant in Japan two years ago, toxicity levels have tripled and sea life has suffered record losses...
In other news, Vancouver business owners in the downtown East Side have banned together with a petition to close down the Thompson House homeless shelter after a string of murders in the area related to trouble amongst the homeless have

left six dead and many citizens concerned for their safety... "

As she spoke I remembered the how the Watchman predicted that it would end up with the city turning on the homeless.

She continued, "We now take you to a live interview with Axel Benjamin..."

The screen split in two and Axel Benjamin, the Watchman's key suspect, now stared me in the face. He was a young and handsome man, not to mention rich. It was hard to believe that someone of that stature could orchestrate such an intricate conspiracy...but something about him during the interview made me think twice. He just seemed so slimy and disingenuous. I know that describes most young, rich people, but still. It just didn't feel right.

"These murders come at a time when your company, Axel Industries, has begun to shape a new and brighter future for the downtown East Side. Do you feel that these killings may overshadow what you are trying to accomplish?"

He responded with the confident positivity of a politician. "Not at all, Audrey. In fact, it only emphasizes the point that the time for change in this area has come. For too long the area has been plagued with gangs, drugs and crime. The people of

Vancouver had every right to be afraid to go down these roads after dark. Axel Industries has a plan to change all this, putting the power back into the hands of the working people of this great city."

That sounded great and all, but he forgot to mention that the only people who were murdered *were* homeless people. I didn't buy it. And I spent most my time lying to people so I would know a liar when I see one. That's when I saw the man with the bruised jaw standing behind Axel. The man from the picture the Watchman had showed me the previous night... Jeremy Stands. He really *was* working for Axel. All this put together seemed too fishy to overlook. Maybe he really *was* using muscle to get rid of the Thompson House. It wouldn't be the first time a super-rich guy got caught doing something terrible.

I decided that I would meet the Watchman that night as he requested and follow him down whatever rabbit-hole he was trying to drag me into. If I could be the one to break this story not only would my conscious be cleared of my part in the Watchman's false accusation, but I would be the reporter who was responsible for taking down one of the biggest business moguls in the city...Like Deep Throat in the Watergate scandal. It would be instant fame!

I impatiently watched the clock drag through the day until finally the sun had set below the skyline and the night was born over downtown's glowing street lamps and neon marquees. I again dressed up in my darkest clothes, grabbed my camera and tape recorder and headed out to my car. The closer I got to East Hastings the more police vehicles I saw driving by, red and blue lights lit up the night as they passed. The area was under pretty heavy guard, I wondered if the Watchman would come out at all tonight.

I arrived just after ten, parked a couple blocks down from the shelter and got out. I walked under the wood planked scaffold that separate the sidewalk from the vast surrounding construction zone. The whole area was like this now; under construction. It was like a bomb went off. I couldn't believe all the buildings they tore down. Besides the low-income apartments they also got rid of Murphy's Pub, the place you could get a pint for only three bucks. But the taps were always pretty dirty and you could taste it. I went there from time to time when I was short on cash or if I wanted to score some coke. Now it was rubble. The holes for the new condos had already been dug. Everywhere you looked, AXEL INDUSTRIES was on some sign or poster. It felt strange, like Hastings had lost some of its soul…Like it had been defeated.

As I crossed the street I noticed Marie, the little old panhandler I first interviewed about the murders. She was drunk I think, limping more than normal and kind of falling over her cane. Suddenly, from out of the shadows, a dark figure emerged...It was The Hooded Killer.

I screamed out to her, "Marie! Look out!"

I watched as he turned to me and then to her. She was far too drunk to hear me. He swooped in, grabbed her by the root of her hair and threw her into the alleyway. They both disappeared from my sight. I bolted as fast as I could across the road. I don't know what made me forgo the thought of my own safety but all I knew was no matter what, Marie wasn't going to be another one of those victims on the news for Audrey Mason to jab on about the next morning. Not her. I couldn't let it happen. I *wouldn't* let it happen!

I ducked in the alley with my fists cocked, but I was too late. I felt my knees buckle and my stomach turn as I watched the Killer pull his knife from out of her chest. She dropped to the floor, dead, and then he turned his attention to me. Poking out from the shadow of the hood was a bruised jaw. The Watchman was right. The Killer was Jeremy Stands, Axel's bodyguard.

"It's you," he snarled. "The one who took the picture…Way to go. Couldn't have framed the Watchman without it."

I felt my face get hot and fists started to shake. "You killed her! You sick fuck! You killed her! How could you do that?!"

"Yeah I did…It felt nice. Now it's your turn. Sorry, no photos." He grabbed my camera, which hung around my neck, snapped it from its strap and smashed it on the floor.

But I didn't care about the five hundred dollar camera that he just smashed. I didn't care I was about to die, a 23 year old in the prime of his life…well okay, maybe not *prime*. I was out of shape and unemployed, but *still*. All I cared about was that this *asshole* just murdered an innocent woman. No matter how many teeth she had, no matter what she did for money, no matter how she chose to live her life…she was an innocent girl. And he took her life away. He had to pay. Evil fucks like him needed to pay. It wasn't about money or fame anymore, it wasn't about getting laid anymore…As I stood there facing down the Killer and his blood stained shiv, only one thing mattered… Revenge.

We stood there, staring each other down, each man waiting for the other to make his first move. Marie's body lied behind him near the fence, limp and lifeless on the concrete. I have to admit, I was scared…but even more than that, I was angry. I was livid. This piece of shit-ass fucker-dick fart had to die.

"What kind of person is willing to die for a bum?" the Killer snarled.

"Fuck you," I said.

"You're not going to be fucking anyone. Not when I'm through cutting you up."

Almost on cue, I heard the Watchman's raspy voice coming from behind Stands. "Leave him alone, Stands," he said. "It's over."

Passing sirens from a few streets over lit up the alley enough to see the Watchman above Stands, crouched on a fence. He leaped from his position and landed in the alley between Stands and myself. The Hooded Killer smiled, "I was hoping to run into you again…You fucked up my chin."

He darted at the Watchman with the blade, missing but getting close enough to cut a hole through the sleeve of his leather jacket. The Watchman retaliated with a hard kick that sent Stands back a few steps. He snarled and regained his footing.

The Watchman called out to me, "Take the girl! I'll take care of him."

As they threw fists back and forth, I ran to Marie and picked her up in my arms. My adrenaline and her years of drug use had made her an easy haul to carry. I raced out of the alley into the streets and didn't look back. Running up the block against the rain I screamed for help, but the people on the streets just stared at me blankly. Afraid or unwilling, I wasn't sure. Either way they weren't trying to help me. *Bunch of assholes*, I thought. *Grow some fucking balls*.

My screams and the fact that I was carrying a dead woman finally got the attention of two cops standing by their squad car on the corner up the block. However, I didn't get the response I was looking for. They drew their guns and pointed them at me. One screamed, "Drop the girl! Now!"

I stared to speak, but the other cop cut me off, "Now, asshole!"

Before I had finished leaning down to rest her on the pavement one of them shoved his knee into my side which sent me to the floor. Marie's dead eyes stared blankly back at me. The other officer raced over and put his knee into my back, cuffing my hands behind me as he read me my rights. I screamed and cursed that they had the wrong guy and I was just trying to help, but they didn't listen. "You got a right to remain silent, kid," said the cop. "You should use it."

They stuck me in the back of the squad car and that's where I stayed until we got back to the police station. No one said anything to me until they had me in the interrogation room. They didn't bring me water, they didn't give me a phone call, nothing. They searched me, took my I.D. and left me in the room for about another hour before the detective finally came in. He gave me a small smile and a nod. "You are Jake Dunlop, correct?"

"Yes…"

"I see," said the detective. "Well, I'm Detective Armstrong and I will be kind of going through tonight's events with you so we can kind of figure out what's going on here. How did you know the victim?"

"Her name's Marie…I didn't know her. Well, I had talked to her once before. She was a panhandler by the Cambie."

"She was stabbed up pretty bad. Did you see what happened?"

"Yes, I saw it all! I tried telling the cops, they didn't listen! It was Jeremy Stands! He's the killer you guys have been looking for! The one behind the Hasting's murders!"

He took a calm sip of his coffee, "He's this Watchman guy?"

"No! Not the Watchman...Listen...*I'm* the one who took that picture that was published in the Province with the Watchman standing over Jeremy Stands, who was the guy in the fucki—" I took a breath to calm down. "The guy in the hood... They got the story all wrong, it was Stands who attacked the homeless guy and it was the Watchman who saved him."

"Stands? Who is that?"

"Jeremy Stands," I said. "He works for Axel Benjamin."

"Axel Benjamin? Of Axel Industries?"

I swear this guy wasn't too sharp for a detective. "Yes," I replied. "Him."

I told him all about Axel's plan to use his henchman to drive the Thompson house to selling their land but I could tell he wasn't buying it. Luckily for me, it seemed his suspicion of me being the one who killed Marie had evaporated to a point where he was willing to let me go home to sleep through what little of the night was left.

****

 The sun was breaking through the horizon as the cab dropped me in front of my building. My body ached but my mind raced, wondering what had happened between Jeremy Stands and the Watchman after I left. Did Stands get away? Or did The Watchman kill him? A part of me hoped the Watchman *had* killed him. For what he did to Marie and the others, he didn't deserve to live...*And,* that asshole smashed my camera.

I dragged myself into the apartment and dropped on the couch. As I did something outside on the balcony caught my eye. Something was shining, reflecting the sun rise into the apartment. I got up from my seat and walked over to the window. My eyes went wide when I noticed what it was...

I ripped open the balcony sliding door and picked up the small plastic bag that was tied to the handrail. It contained three things: The first was my tape recorder; how I had dropped it I had no idea. I thought maybe when I was bending over to lift up Marie it had fallen out of my pocket or something. The second item was the shiv that belonged to the Hooded Killer; it was still stained with Marie's blood on the edge. The third item was a note. I closed the door behind me and pulled out the note.

It read, "I gave your recorder a listen. It seems you're a better reporter than I thought...I thought this knife full of his fingerprints and the victim's blood might help your case."

I didn't know what he meant about the recorder, not until I pressed play and heard the Hooded Killer's voice on the other end saying, "It's you!...The one who took the picture. Way to go. Couldn't have framed the Watchman without it."

I pressed pause and felt a grin stretch up my cheeks until I busted out into a laugh. I don't know how, I don't know why, but by some crazy stroke of luck...I had recorded everything. I had Jeremy Stands admitting to the murders *on tape*! And his murder weapon wrapped up neatly in a Ziploc bag!

"I got you now, you slimy fuck!" I screamed.

****

The next day I picked up my car that had been parked down the street from the shelter and drove to the Cambie to meet Johnny at his post. He finished up with one of his customers and nodded me over. "What'll it be?" he asked.

"No weed today." I said. "I need you to come with me."

He chuckled softly, "Get the fuck outta here."

"I'm serious. You're coming with me. I need your help."

He took his hand out of his pockets and gave me a little push on the shoulder, "And why the fuck am I going to help you? First you come here for a fucking interview and now you want to go on a date? I sell weed, not friendship...Fuck off."

"This will help your business, I promise!"

His blank stare told me he wasn't sold.

I continued, "Okay, so you know how they're re-building this whole area to make it nice and shit...What do you think is going to happen to you when all the new shit goes up? You think they're going to let you sit here and sell dope? If you come with me now I can make it so that all this re-construction bullshit stops and you can go on selling weed forever."

That got his attention. "And how the fuck are you going to do that?" he asked.

* *

We pulled up to the Vancouver Sun building and Johnny walked into the lobby while I waited outside. If my plan was going to work, things had to go just right. About three or four minutes later Johnny came whipping out the front doors, the Somalian security guard from the front desk chasing him through the front terrace. Seizing my opportunity I entered the lobby and got to the elevators before the security got back in the building. Johnny had played his role as a distraction perfectly...I was in.

I entered the main office and darted for Mr. Dennis' office but Diana spotted me quickly and sprang up from her desk. I could tell she was proud of herself for actually catching me this time.

"Go away," she said.

"Please, Diana. I—"

She cut me off, "I told you I don't want to talk to you."

"I know, I know...I'm here to see your dad, I need to talk to him. It's important."

She raised her voice, "He doesn't want to see you! People make appointments; they don't just barge in to the office and demand to see him! Who the fuck do you think you are? You got some balls coming in here!"

I smiled, I couldn't help it. She was really pretty when she got angry. Suddenly the door to Mr. Dennis' office swung open and there he stood, just as pissed and stressed out as the last time I saw him.

"What's all the racket out here?! I'm trying to—"he stopped in his tracks as he saw me standing there next to his fuming daughter. "You! Again you sneak into my office?!"

I pleaded, waving around my Ziploc bag with the knife and recorder, "Mr. Dennis, it's important, I swear! I have the story! I have evidence!"

By this time the whole office had stopped what they were doing.

He shook his head, "That's it, I've had it. I'm calling security!"

I yelled at him as he went back into his office, "Mr. Dennis, if you call security now you'll miss out on an opportunity to completely discredit the Province!"

He stopped at the door. After a moment of thought, he nodded me over. I followed him into the office, grinning at Diana as I passed. He closed the door behind us.

After playing him the tape of Jeremy Stands confession we agreed that the Vancouver Sun would get the exclusive on this story with the promise that I would in turn receive a job as a staff reporter on the paper.

I left the office with a smile, the last thing Diana expected to see. "What's with you?" she said as I skipped by her desk.

"Well, Diana...Your dad just gave me a job. I guess we'll be seeing a lot of each other from now on. I'll see you real soon!"

Yeah, she looked pretty when she was angry. That day she looked absolutely beautiful.

The story went to print and it made headlines all over. Not only was Jeremy Stands arrested but Axel Benjamin was also indicted on conspiracy. However, like most rich and powerful men, he beat the charges. Stands didn't do so well...He got life in prison.

Though the reconstruction of the Lower East Side continued, the Thompson House remained alive and the Watchman's name was cleared. I haven't seen the Watchman since that night in the alley but

I know he's out there somewhere...watching. And when the day ever comes that Vancouver needs him again, I have no doubt he'll be there to answer the call. I know because I'll be right behind him.

You know why?

Because I'm Jake Dunlop...I'm a fucking reporter, bitch.

Story Two: Rise of the Hipster

Ah, Halloween—it's the time of year where girls dressing like Homer Street hookers is considered festive, where eggs become artillery for angst ridden adolescence terrorizing the city on skateboards and scooters, and where the "don't take candy from strangers" practice literally walks out the door for one night of magical hedonistic fun…

What's up, bitches! Jake Dunlop here. It's been two years since we last spoke but I'm *back* with another butt-clenching tale from the infamous Hastings Hero. That's right! The man in the bandana, the Watchman himself, returned to save the city of Vancouver from peril once again from an evil dick known to many of the city's residents as only, The Hipster!

Not too much has changed in the two years since we left off; I'm still a reporter for the Sun (Woop! Woop!), I also finally convinced Diana to go out on a date with me, but after a few of those she ended it pretty abruptly. She said I was "detached" from reality, whatever that means. I think it was because I chose cartoons over sex a couple times…What? They were new episodes!

It was October and, in addition to being a month of loose morality, it also happened to be election month. And while most people can choose to ignore this tedious time in Canadian life, I, as a reporter, was paid to care. Everyday some new piece of candidate gossip flooded the news room, conservative this and liberal that—it drove me fucking nuts. I tried my best to become numb to it. To me, if you're a politician, no matter what party you're in, you are a douche. You have to be a douche, really; your whole job depends on manipulation, telling people what they want to hear, looking like the person they want to see and being able to sway the topic at hand, whatever it may be, in your favor and out of your competitions. Meanwhile, the promises made to the people are empty because the time in office is mainly spent focusing on the agenda of the big corporations who funded their campaign. Corporations like that which belonged to Axel Benjamin, the *king* of the douche.

He was still rich as fuck by the way. By now everyone had forgotten about his involvement in the Hooded Killer scandal and he was shaking hands and kissing babies as if it never even happened. He was a financier for the Conservative campaign in Vancouver and off limits for scrutiny being that the Sun was a widely known right wing publication. If Axel Benjamin was high on meth, raping babies in the middle of Robson—You wouldn't hear about it in the pages of the Sun. Not during election season anyway.

So you can imagine how *super* stoked I was when Mr. Dennis, Diana's father and my boss, assigned me to cover the Conservative rally down at Victory Square which was hosted and sponsored by Axel Industries.

"Come on, do I have to?" I whined. "That guy is a dick."

"I don't have time to argue with you today," he said behind a stack of papers. "Please, Jake...Just get it done."

"Okay, Chief. Just for you, I'll go."

He waved me off and went back to his papers, "I'm flattered. Now fuck off, I'm busy."

I left him to his work, closing the office door behind me as I made my exit. I walked over to Diana's desk and sat on the corner of it as she was finishing up a phone call. She hung up and looked at me, "Fuck off, Jake. I'm busy."

"Geese. The apple doesn't fall far from the tree, does it?"

"What do you want?"

"I just wanted to let you know that I will be covering the Conservative rally at Victory Square today, which means my night is looking pretty free if you wanted to get some dinner with this reporter."

She laughed, running her hands through her hair. "I'll have to gracefully decline, I already have a date tonight. In fact, that was just him I was talking to on the phone."

"Oh, he can use a phone? He's a smart cookie this one. Is he the "attached" to reality type you're so drawn to?"

She nodded. "Very much so. He's a politician."

"Fuck off..."

"Excuse me?"

"Nothing..."

"He'll actually be the speaker at the rally you're going to. He's the candidate for our region."

"What's his name?"

"You should know his name. What kind of newsman are you?"

"Obviously not a good one. I thought Stephen Harper was the conservative candidate."

"Do you know how politics even work? We elect the party, not the person. Different regions have different candidates and those people make up the seats in parliament. Whoever has the most seats voted into parliament becomes the elected leaders."

"That's fantastic stuff...So what's his name?"

"Georgio Mochella."

"Georgio? That's a stupid name."

"Armani had it."

"*Armani had it*," I said, mimicking her in an animated rendition of how stupid I thought she sounded.

She rolled her eyes, "Okay, you've wasted enough of my time. Bye, little man."

I left her to her business and headed out into the city. I liked to complain to Mr. Dennis when he sent me out on the field but I did that mainly just to fuck with him. For some reason seeing him stress out put a smile on my face. Truthfully, I enjoyed any chance I got to be set free in the beautiful landscape of Vancouver. The warmth of summer had recently left us and a cool fall breeze had taken its place. Short shorts and tank tops had been replaced with yoga pants and Uggs. The smell of pumpkin spice lattes seeped through Yaletown as the orange and yellow leaves began to fall and pictures of ghosts and goblins were starting to appear in the shop windows.

 When I arrived at Victory Square they were in the midst of setting up sound and lights while the press started to arrive. I had some time to kill so being that I was running dangerously low on my weed supply I decided to head over to the Cambie and see Johnny at his corner.

"What's up, what's up, my ninja?" I said, putting my hand up for a high five.

He nodded his head, his hands remaining firmly buried in his sweater pockets. "What'll it be?"

I put down my hand. "An eighth, please."

He reached out and handed me a Ziploc bag in return for a pair of twenties.

Then he looked up to me, concerned. "Hey, you're a reporter, right?"

"Fuck yeah," I said.

"Do you know anything about what happened at PharmCorp last night?"

PharmCorp was the billion dollar pharmaceutical lab that took the place of the old Army Navy on Hastings. It was part of Axel Benjamin's attempt to "clean up" east Hastings. After the whole Hooded Killer incident, Axel used the construction of PharmCorp to his advantage by adding a methadone clinic for addicts to receive clean needles and treatment for their illnesses. An act of kindness like that put any question of his character out of the public mind.

"No, what happened?" I asked.

"Not sure. I saw a couple unmarked cars fishing around for about an hour before they left. I found it a little suspicious. "

"Haven't heard much, but I'll look into it."

"Do I get a reward for the tip?"

I shook my head. "Not today, Johnny. Not today."

I went back up to the street where by now the press had set up, the podium was erect and the speaker, Diana's honey bunny Georgio Mochella, was already in the midst of his speech.

Behind Georgio was playboy Axel Benjamin in a black and white striped suit, looking like fucking Beetlejuice or something. As per usual he had about ten pounds of lube in his hair and that shit eating grin of entitlement pasted on his face.

Beside him, two older men stood with solem faces. They were dressed impeccably well. Beside them, there was this absolute sweetheart of a girl who had me locked on target from the second I laid eyes on her. She had this extremely cute, dorky thing about her. I liked that though, I thought simplicity was sexy as fuck. I was surprised though, that I was so taken by a blonde. I'm usually a dead sucker for a brunette, like Diana, but this girl had it. Whatever *it* was, she was glowing in it. Though I kept telling myself to focus on Georgio, my focus would only last briefly before it drifted over to this cute blonde clumsily brushing the windblown hair out of her face.

I suppose I caught the usual conservative jargon; "We're going to balance the budget with low spending!", "We'll create jobs with low corporate taxes!", "We're going to keep this country safe and secure from terrorists threats against our freedom!" And with every exclamation point came a thunderous applause from the crowd of right wingers. The fact he was so adored only made me more jealous he'd most likely be sticking it to Diana later in the evening.

In the midst of cursing Georgio under my breath I turned my head to notice a large crowd coming over from the Vapor Lounge across the street. The stoner mob looked rowdy and carried signs with anti-right slogans like, "Adolf Harper!", "C-51 is slavery!", "Weed is not a crime!" and I think I even saw one that said, "Harper eats babies!"

At the front of the pack stood an *ultra*-hipster. The Hipster of all hipsters. He had long greasy hair, glasses that I'm betting were not prescription, the trademark hipster beard and fully tattooed arms under a sleeveless Guns n' Roses shirt–new, but faded purposely to make it look old and worn. His pants were a pumpkin colored pair of corduroy's and his boots were made of some kind of reptile skin, complete with *actual fucking spurs*. One by one the heads at the rally turned and saw what I was seeing. Even Georgio stopped his speech as the stoner crew surrounded us.

One of the Hipster's cronies holding a small speaker handed the Hipster a microphone with one hand while he turned on the amp with the other. There was a brief shriek of feedback and then the Hipster spoke, "Good people of Vancouver! Do not believe the lies told to you by this Hoodlum of Harper! He is just another soldier in the regime that has plagued this country for the last decade! I bet he tells you that Bill C-51 is for your "protection". That we need to spy on Canadians in order to stop the "terrorist threat against our freedom". But did you know that you're more likely to be killed by a moose than a terrorist?"

"Yeah, you're more likely to die from a moose!" yelled one of the sign wielding protesters.

"Yeah, you idiots!" yelled another.

One of the conservative supporters yelled, "Go home, you're high!" and everyone on the right and even some reporters started to laugh.

The Hipsters face went red. "Typical right wing ignorance! The conservatives want you to believe that cannabis is just a street drug that makes you stupid because they believe in the privatization of the prison system that profits from sending innocent people to jail! The Conservatives want to deny the proof that cannabis oil cures cancer so that their investors like Axel Benjamin and PharmCorp can make record profits selling cancer treatments that don't work!"

"Fuck PharmCorp!" yelled a protester.

"Weed cures cancer, you idiots!" yelled another.

Axel Benjamin cut in front of Mochella, who was at a loss for words, and spoke on the microphone,

"Sir, to speak of PharmCorp in such a way as you have is a falsehood. The fact is that PharmCorp is on the verge of many astronomical advances in the field of medical science and they do It all with the goal of making life better for the Canadian citizen. No one can testify to this more than our new Head of Research, Dr. Susan Drake..."

Axel extended his hand to the dorky blonde I had been eyeing. She waved and smiled uncomfortably. The conservative supporters whistled and cheered.

"What good are medical breakthroughs when they are only allotted to the rich?" The Hipster asked. "This election vote NDP and end the decade long rape of our country!"

"NDP! Whoo!" yelled a voice behind him.

"Weed cures cancer, you idiots!" yelled another.

The crowd marched off towards the Hastings Warehouse and those of us left stood around scratching our heads. Mochella finished his speech but it was clear even he was trying to piece together what just had happened. I didn't let it bother me too much; people say all kinds of dumb stuff when they're high. Unfortunately, the press doesn't care if you're high or not and judging by the thumbs frantically typing away on their Blackberry's, it was clear the Hipster would be the next piece of political gossip flying around the newsrooms.

While the other reporters were busy doing *that*, I thought I would use my time more wisely by taking this opportunity to interview that cute blonde doctor...for, y'know, info and stuff...

I walked to where she stood at the arch of the hill and introduced myself, "Dr. Susan Drake? I'm Jake Dunlop, I'm a reporter. I was wondering if I could have a moment of your time?"

She brushed her bangs from her eyes, "Oh, uh, sure..."

"That guy was pretty nutty, eh?"

"Yeah, weird...So, um, why do you want to talk to me?"

"Well, I'm doing an article on the rally and I thought if I could find out why PharmCorp chooses to be such a large campaign contributor to this party...If I could find out why someone like you believes in the conservative party, I think it could give a more honest look at politics for young readers who feel out of touch with the system."

She thought about it for a second and then said, "Well, Axel Industries is partners with PharmCorp, they fund a lot of our research. I'm here in place of my father because, well, he's dead. I'm not really too political, but Axel asked me to be here and he pays the bills so..." Then she caught herself mid-sentence, "Shit—I mean—don't write that down, I don't want to get in any trouble. It would probably be best if you didn't print any of that."

"Well I would hate to see you get fired on my account," I said. "Although, you can't deny what a juicy little headline that would be, "Conservative main investor secretly politically apathetic." That could be a huge blow to the party's reputation. We'd sell a bunch of papers, I'd get a promotion, and maybe move into a bigger condo...I'm really going out on a limb here for you. But, why don't we go for dinner tonight and we'll try this again. It'll give you some time to think of a reason why the Conservatives are just *the best*."

She gave me a half smile, "Are you...blackmailing me for a date?"

I laughed, "That depends. Do you find it charming or creepy?"

Now she laughed, "I'm still trying to figure that one out...But okay, Jake. How about Guilt & Co. at nine."

"Guilt and Co. Nine. You got it."

"Okay, Jake I'll see you there," she said before she walked off, *obviously* under the spells of my irresistible charm.

I stood and watched her pretty little bum walk away. I was impressed with myself, I won't lie. But since no one was going to be buying papers with articles about my skills with the ladies, my next course of action was to do some hard-core sleuthing and find out just who this Hipster guy was.

From what I knew so far, he was pro-NDP and had a lot of pothead supporters so I spent the rest of the day between the BCMP headquarters and dispensaries in the area trying to find answers. It turned out he was a pretty popular guy. His real name was Simon Baker, people knew him from different cannabis rallies and activists groups. They said he was like a preacher; more often than not you would find him surrounded by peers, giving speeches on socialist philosophy like some sort of Inked-up Jesus. But of all the people that knew and talked to Simon Baker, no one had any information on his whereabouts before the last two years. It seemed he just appeared out of nowhere.

I thought maybe I could find more answers at the NDP office in Burnaby. The lady who greeted me had been very warm and kind until I asked her about Simon Banks and told her what happened at the rally.

"We've been getting calls about him all day," she grumbled. "He volunteered with us for a while but he was asked to leave about a month ago. He was crazy, getting into fights all the time...He felt the party wasn't left enough. A real violent socialist, that one. If he is going around causing problems waving the NDP flag, I assure you, we knew nothing of it."

I thanked the lady and left. I had enough information to write my article. I got home, showered, changed and headed over to Guilt & Co. to meet Susan. When I arrived she was sitting at a lounge table looking like a sweet little angel over the candle light. I walked passed the jazz band and sat down at the lounge table with Susan.

"You came!" she said, almost surprised.

"Yeah, sorry I'm late. I was standing outside trying to decide if I should turn around and run or not."

She stared at me blankly.

"I'm kidding," I said. "You look amazing by the way. I never had a doctor that looked like you before. All my doctors were old guys with low monotone voices and white stuff at the side of their mouth."

She laughed.

"Rich *and* pretty," I continued. "Life must be tough, huh?"

"Well, there's more to a book than its cover," she said. "Everyone's got a story."

"And that's why I'm here." I said. "I want to know everything. So how did it come to be that someone as young as you is so entangled with the likes of political parties and Axel Benjamin?"

"I'm not that young. I'm 35."

"Get the fuck out of here...Were you cryogenically frozen or something?"

She laughed. I felt good, I got a couple laughs right off the bat; it helped me loosen up a bit.

The waitress took my order and Susan told me her story. Her father died three years ago in an explosion at the old PharmCorp building. He left her everything; his research, his shares and majority control of his company–everything.

"So," I said, "This whole campaign trail is what, a necessary evil to appease your stockholders?"

"*Off* the record? Yes." she replied with a smile, "The only reason I am involved with politics is politics. What about you? Are you political?"

Before I could make up a lie about how totally political I was, there was a loud frightened scream at the front of the restaurant. The band stopped playing, the singer stopped singing and the lounge waitress stopped dead in her tracks, tray full of drinks and all. Three men stood at the front entrance holding shotguns and wearing Stephen Harper Halloween masks.

"Good evening, ladies and gentlemen!" The front man said from under his plastic mask.

He fired a shot into the ceiling to show he wasn't fucking around. People started to scream. The other two gunmen kept their weapons pointed at the patrons while the front man zig zagged through the lounge like a slithering snake hunting its prey. His voice had a familiar tone, but when I saw the brown corduroy's and the lizard skin boots, it gave him away. It was the Hipster under that mask. I knew it.

"I'm here for Dr. Susan Drake!" he shouted. "Everybody co-operate and no one will get hurt. If anyone tries to intervene or call the police, you will be shot!"

Susan gasped, "Oh my god..."

"I won't let him take you," I whispered. But it was an empty promise. Before I had any time to think of some heroic plan the Hipster was standing over our table with his shotgun pointed directly at my face.

"Bingo," he said.

He pulled Susan out of her seat by her arm and dragged her screaming through the dining room while the two other gunmen kept their shotguns in my face. I was helpless.

In just a moment they were gone back out the front enterance and the patrons of the restaurant, feeling safer now, began to chatter among themselves and break out their phones. I wasn't about to see my date get kidnapped in front of my very eyes and do nothing about it so I threw forty bucks on the table and ran out the restaurant after them.

As I ran up the front steps and out onto the lantern lit, cobblestone streets I saw a black Cadillac speeding away. I started to run after it but something grabbed me from behind and tackled me to the ground.

"Get the fuck off me!" I screamed as I struggled with my unknown assailant. I managed to flip over onto my back and that's when I saw him. "Holy shit! It's you!" I said.

The toque, the face covered in a black bandana, the scarred face, the punk rock leather jacket...There's only one guy I knew with that ensemble...The Hastings Watchman!

He shook me. "Are you working for them? Did you set her up?!"

"No! I swear! We were just eating dinner and then..."

He cut me off, "Come with me."

I got to my feet and followed him down the alley. When we turned the corner there was a white cube van parked by the fence. He threw me the keys.

"Get in, you're driving," he said.

I chuckled, "What is this, like, the Watchman Wagon or something?"

"I stole it," he said plainly.

"Just fucking great," I said, opening the door and getting in the front seat. "I'm going to jail tonight, aren't I?"

I started the engine and slammed it in reverse until we had backed out of the alley onto the main roads. Then I punched it into drive and headed after the black Cadillac.

"I don't see them," I said as we sped down the road. "I think we lost them."

"Keep driving," the Watchman replied. "I know where they're going."

"Who are these guys? What do they want with her?"

"About a week ago there was a break in at PharmCorp. It was made to look like a morphine grab...But there was another drug, a drug called Rejuvicell, that went missing. Dr. Susan Drake is the only one who knows the protocol for administering it properly. I believe the man who abducted her, a nutcase named Simon Banks, wants to administer the Rejuvicell on himself."

"I knew it was the fucking Hipster!" I yelled. "He wore a mask, but I knew...So then what? What happens? What does this Rejuvicell do?"

"Turn left here, get on the highway…It's based on the salamanders ability to create new cells and replaced damaged ones. The purpose of the drug was to repair damaged or ruptured flesh and organs from the inside, without the need for surgery. If properly consumed, this would give the recipient the ability of extraordinary healing and strength. A man could recover from multiple gunshot wounds in a matter of minutes."

"So in the hands of someone like the Hipster?"

"Bad fucking news," he replied.

A chill ran down my spine and my foot pressed heavy on the gas. If we didn't get to him before he dosed the Rejuvicell, this fight was going to get a lot more difficult.

The Watchman directed me to an industrial warehouse on the edge of Burnaby and Surrey, under the Port Mann Bridge. We pulled up with our headlights off and parked far enough away to keep hidden in the shadows.

"Okay, stay here," said the Watchman.

"Fuck that!" I said, "That's my date he's got in there!"

"Stay!" he barked.

I huffed and sat back in my seat while he opened the passenger side door and vanished into the darkness. After about ten minutes of gritting my teeth I decided I was going in, with or without the blessings of the Watchman. If anything happened to Susan while I was just sitting around in a van doing nothing, I would never be able to forgive myself.

I got out of the van and started to creep along the shadows, staying out of the light shining down from the front lot. That's when I heard the sound of two gunshots coming from inside the warehouse. Then...silence.

I took two more slow steps forward and that's when the front entrance window exploded open, shattering pieces of glass all over the pavement along with a large, dark blob that I quickly recognized to be the Watchman. I jumped back and hid behind a dip in the wall. The Hipster walked out of the shattered remains of the window. His mask was off now. In his hands was a shotgun. He pointed at the Watchman and fired off two shots. **BAM! BAM!**

The Watchman fell to the floor...dead.

The Hipster let out a loud, "Ha!" and called over to his hoodlums, "Leave the girl! She has fulfilled her purpose! Now it is time for Phase 2!"

I watched carefully as The Hipster and his goons got back into the black Cadillac and drove away. As soon as the coast was clear I ran inside for Susan. She was standing over a dental chair next to what looked to be some sort of make-shift lab, like something you would see in a meth kitchen or a psycho rapist's basement. She was shaking and in tears.

I lightly touched her shoulder, "Susan, are you okay?"

"It's happening again..." she mumbled, wiping away some tears from her cheek.

"What? What's happening again?" I asked.

"I wish my father never even invented that stupid drug...he'd still be alive."

"Wait," I said, "Are you saying that the Rejuvicell had something to do with the explosion that killed your father?"

Her eyes went wide and she took a cautious step back, "H-H-How did you know what the drug is called? He never went public with his findings; no one knows about that drug but my father and me….And how did you know that I would be here? You aren't working for those guys who kidnapped me, are you? Is that how they knew I would be at Guilt & Co.? Is it?!"

"No! Susan, I swear!" I went to reach for her but she pulled away.

"Get away from me!" she screamed. "Just leave me alone!"

She ran out of the warehouse and into the night. I knew she was too upset to be reasoned with so I let her go. I walked over to the shattered window in the front and looked out…The Watchman's body was gone. It made me think back to that night I saw him get stabbed by the Hooded Killer. He somehow survived that time too. How could this guy take two shells to the chest?…and live?

I thought about everything that had happened in the last twenty four hours and who knows, maybe I was just tired and not thinking clearly, but I knew there was more to the story than I was seeing. Something deeper, a bigger picture and whatnot…I was determined to find out what that picture was. But first I needed to smoke a bowl and get some sleep. It had been one long ass fucking day….

****

"Jake! Get in here! You're thirty minutes late!" yelled the Chief from inside his office. "Are you trying to get fired?"

Diana sat at her desk with a grin across her face as she typed away on her computer. I gave her my best "*Har, har har*. I'm glad you find this so funny" face.

"No, sir," I replied. "In fact when you hear what I have for you, I might just get a promotion. I was at the library all morning looking for information on Dr. Stewart Drake and—"

"Stewart Drake?" he said, "What do I care about a Stewart Drake? I told you to write an article on the Georgio Mochella rally!"

"With all due respect, sir...Fuck Georgio Mochella."

The grin from Diana's face dropped, replaced with a cold glare as I stepped passed her into Mr. Dennis' office, closing the door behind me.

"I went to the rally," I continued. "This Hipster by the name of Simon Banks came and hijacked it. At first, he seemed like an NDP supporter but I followed up with the local office and it turns out he was kicked out for being too left...and *violent* too.

Then later in the night he showed up at Guilt & Co. and kidnapped my date!"

His head perked up from his desk, "You witnessed the kidnapping? The men in the Harper masks? I already have Donaldson on it. What do you have?"

I told him about the break in at PharmCorp and the stolen Rejuvicell, how the Hipster administered it to himself and shot the Watchman before he escaped. To my surprise, Chief didn't love it as much as I thought he would.

"Are you serious?" he asked. "This is what you have for me? A secret drug that makes you invincible? A murder where the victim gets up and walks away? Do you have any proof of any of this? We're not some cheap tabloid, you know! People expect us to actually back up what we publish! And the Watchman?! What's he doing back after all this time? What's he got to do with this?!"

"The doctor told me no one knew about the drug but her and her father...Dr. Stewart Drake, the PharmCorp Head of Research who died in an explosion a few years back. But maybe he didn't die...Maybe before the explosion he took the Rejuvicell and survived. I mean, why would the Watchman chase after this girl if she didn't mean something to him? How is it possible that the

Watchman keeps getting stabbed and shot—and lives?"

"So what are you saying?" Mr. Dennis asked.

"The Watchman is Stewart Drake—Susan's father!"

"That's all fine and well, Jake...but what the *fuck* does it have to do with elections?!"

"Uh...Nothing, I guess?"

"Exactly! Nothing!" he screamed. "Now I want an article on my desk before deadline, you hear me? No Watchman crap, no secret miracle serum—the conservative rally and that's it, got it?!"

I smiled and agreed. Then I left and closed the door behind me.

"Sounded pretty heated in there," Diana said as I passed.

"Just another day at the office," I replied.

"Aren't you going to ask me how my date was?" she asked.

I spun around, "You know, Diana, did it ever occur to you that I might have other things on my mind other than *you*?"

She recoiled. I could tell she wasn't expecting such a harsh return but fuck it; I didn't have time for our usual flirty bullshit. I grabbed my laptop from my desk and made my way to the door.

On my way out Jonah, one of the new interns, came running towards me in his usual excited and comical manner. I don't know if he thought I was his mentor or something, but he was super interested in the Watchman/Hooded Killer story. He said it made him want to work for the Sun. Personally, I thought he was like an excited puppy at a dog park...but an owner never came to retrieve him.

"Hey, Jake!" he yelled out. "Guess what?"

"Another time, Jonah!" I yelled. Then I was out the door. I tried slamming it behind me but it was one of those "quiet" doors that shut very slowly. That just made me angrier.

****

I went into the coffee spot on Hastings and Cambie to write the article and have a tea. I liked to sit by the window and watch people on the street go by. About an hour in, just as I was finishing up, I saw someone put down their briefcase and sit down at my table through the corner of my eye. When I looked up from the glow of my laptop, there was Axel Banjamin sitting across of me. He smiled as he fixed his cuff link on his maroon suit jacket.

"Mr. Dunlop, it's nice to finally meet you," he said. "I'm sure you know who I am."

I sneered. "Yeah..."

"Good," he said dryly. "Then we can disperse with the displeasure of pretending we don't know each other. We have a mutual friend, Dr. Susan Drake. She was abducted last night while she was in your care."

"I had nothing to do with it," I said.

"Oh, I'm sure you hadn't," he smiled. "But I am sure you would want to see her captors pay for their misdeeds, correct?"

"Yeah. And?"

"Well, it seems with the new found...*gifts* that our enemy possesses it would be quite hard for a man like me or a man like you to do much damage. But there is another who lurks in the shadows of this city that has the same gifts, is there not? A certain vigilante with a fetish for leather?"

"What are you getting at?" I asked.

"I want to give him something...To help. To defeat this...this..."

"Hipster," I added.

He snapped his fingers and smiled, "Yes! This Hipster!"

He picked up his briefcase from his side and opened it up on the table, pulling out and handing me two thick metal bracelet-like objects. They didn't look very impressive.

"What are they?" I asked.

He looked me hard in the eye, "These are thermal mittens. Really, really expensive thermal mittens."

"Pretty shitty mittens," I said. "They don't even cover your hands."

Axel chuckled, "Oh, they cover the hands just fine. But to keep you and this pretty young barista from soiling yourselves, I won't turn them on right here. Just tell the Watchman that there are activation sensors on the left side of each wrist. All he has to do is put his hands like this..." He put his wrists in the shape of an X, "...And the sensors will activate a sonic force field around his fists. The sonic waves emit immensely dangerous pressure which is ideal for blowing steel doors off their hinges...or perhaps Hipsters heads from their bodies."

He slid the cuffs over to me.

"Why are you helping us? What's in it for you?" I asked.

"I can't let you see all my cards, now can I? Let's just say for now that my interest is purely political. To have this discovery in the hands of a left-wing government who platforms on free healthcare...Well, you can see the problem."

"It's always about the money, huh?" I said.

"Not always," he smirked. "Sometimes it's about the power."

Then he closed up his briefcase and left. I stared at the metallic bracelets in front of me. *Sonic force fields, eh?* I thought. I wanted to take them into the alley and test them out...but with all the talk about blowing heads off bodies and all, I thought the first test would be best done by someone who could rejuvenate any exploded limbs.

I put them in my backpack, packed away my laptop and headed back to the Sun building where I handed in my article to Mr. Dennis. He sat in his chair with his reading glasses on, looking it over.

"That's more like it," he said. "Voters need to know about the choices they have in this thing so they can make an informed decision on Election Day."

"Whatever, Chief...Mark my words, something big is about to go down in the city. The Hipster said something about a Phase 2. And when he does whatever he's going to do and every news network and print job in this whole city is covering the story, just remember—you could have had the exclusive before all of them."

"And you just remember that I got bosses too, kid. And they're not necessarily as nice to me as I am to you. If you can get something concrete, I'll run it. Otherwise my hands are tied."

I left his office to see Diana at her desk staring me down. "In a better mood?" she asked.

"Yeah...no...I don't know. Sorry, I didn't mean to snap on you earlier. I've had a crazy couple days. There's this socialist extremist who stole a drug that he used on himself to become, basically, fucking invincible, he kidnapped my date who now hates me because she thinks I had something to do with it and now Axel Benjamin just gave me a fucking hand bomb to give to the Watchman who, by the way, was shot twice in the chest and lived...Now the bad guy is planning something big against the city and I don't know where or when. I probably won't until it's too late either."

"Wow…" she said.

"Yeah…Stressful shit."

"You…You didn't tell me you were dating someone."

I shook my head, "I think you missed the point of the story, D."

"Well, I'm free tonight if you want to go for a drink and talk about it."

"No Georgio tonight?" I asked.

"He's at the Pacific Rim tonight for the closing campaign dinner…he doesn't like to bring dates to those things."

"Nah…Thanks though. I'm going to try and call this girl and convince her I'm not trying to kill her."

She smiled, "You probably make those calls a lot, don't you?"

"Shut up, D…"

****

I tried Susan a few times but she didn't pick up. I decided I was going to come clean and tell her everything. Even if she didn't believe me, I had to tell her about The Watchman. I had to tell her that her father might still be alive...

I knew she would be at the Conservative campaign wrap up dinner so I figured my best bet was to head over to thePacific Rim where it was being held. I got ready, grabbed my recorder and my camera, as well as the cuffs Axel had given me, and headed out. I knew the security would be tight for such an exclusive event so I grabbed an old press pass I had received for another event at the Rim a few months back. Unfortunately for me, when I got there I quickly learned that there were special press passes made up for this event specifically. So again, I was fucked.

I sat at the lobby bar and had a drink while I thought about any other possible options I had to sneak in that dinner. I was eyeing the bell boy, thinking maybe I could knock him out and take his clothes. Then I quickly dispersed that idea because it was stupid and would never work.

Then, when all seemed lost, a miracle happened. I saw Jonah, the nerdy intern photographer at the Sun, walking out of the conference room like he had a foot long meatball sub up his ass on the way to the bathroom. I ran across the lobby and grabbed him by the shoulder.

His eyes lit up when he saw me. "Hey! Jake!" he cried.

"Hey! Jonah, buddy! Where ya going?" I said.

"I'm going to the bathroom," he said. "Are you staying at the hotel? That's crazy. That's awesome....Like a rock star, right?"

I shook my head, "No, Jonah, listen...I'm going to need that Press Pass you got around your neck there, bud."

Without a word or a question he slid it from around his neck and handed it to me. *Damn*, I thought. *I wasn't expecting much a fight but that was just too easy.*

"I'm not fired am I?" he asked, concerned.

"No. Not at all. In fact, Mr. Dennis sent me to give you the night off for all your hard work and effort. Enjoy the night, go home and be with the girl."

"I'm single," he replied with some disappointment.

"Well there ya go!" I cried, "Go find yourself a nice one and bring her on home!"

He laughed with that donkey sounding laugh of his and said, "Okay, then. Thanks, Jake. You rock. You do good work too by the way. You should get a night off too sometime."

I smiled. "Got it. Thanks, Jonah. See you at the office!"

I left Jonah and raced back to the conference rooms. When I got there I was stopped by security.

"What happened to the other guy?" he asked.

"Stomach upset," I replied. I pulled out my wallet and handed them my I.D. Card from the Sun. "Nothing sinister here, boys. Just covering for a friend."

The security guard opened the door and ushered me in, saying, "Poor guy. He was walking like he shit his pants too."

I entered the dining hall and took a second to gather my surroundings. The press had gathered along the walls on each side of the room, so I found my way in with them so I could blend in. In the middle of the hall were ten tables filled with different investors, politicians, judges and other high society currently in the middle of eating their dinners. At the head of the room a large stage and podium were erected for Georgio Mochella to make his closing speech.

I scanned the tables for Susan and found her sitting just to the left of me at the PharmCorp table. She looked amazing all dolled up. I was stunned. Her blonde hair was tied tightly in a bun which really opened up her face to reveal the bright blue of her eyes and the soft shimmer of her cheek bones. Her forehead was kind of big, but it was cute in her own little dorky way. But even in the extravagance of her gown she looked distant from the conversation and lost in her own thoughts. Beside her sat Axel Benjamin in a perfectly tailored black tuxedo, showering his table with the charm he spewed so naturally. That dick.

At the far end of the room, sitting at the head of the table was Georgio Mochella sitting with his running team and a beautiful girl on his arm that *wasn't* Diana. *How mad would she be if she saw this?* I thought. So I took a couple pictures...just for funzies.

As I smiled to myself in some sort of undeserved vindication, I saw a confrontation taking place at the front door with the same security guard who stopped me on the way in. The altercation became louder and louder, causing everyone to turn and look. Then it got fucking *real*. There was the sound of gunfire. **BAM! BAM! BAM!** Then more screams and more gunfire. **BAM! BAM! BAM!** The doors swung open and two dead security guards dropped to the ground. A pair of reptile skin boots, complete with actual spurs stepped over the corpses into the dining hall. The Hipster had crashed the party.

As he walked in he was followed by about ten more of his goons who spread out through the dining hall shoving guns in people's faces. But it wasn't even the gun wielding maniacs that were the scariest sight...it was the gun wielding maniacs wearing gas masks that really set off the holy shit alarm. Even the Hipster had a gas mask around his face, his hair tied back into a stupid little man-bun. In his hands he held a glowing vile of green gel that I could only assume was not peppermint jelly to add to the lamb.

"My friends!" he shouted. "I hope you have enjoyed your meals tonight! Because it may be the last you ever have! For tonight you will face judgement for your loyalty to Stephen Harper and the Conservative Party! The irreparable damage to the environment, the scandals in the senate, the selling of our country's resources to China, and a foreign policy that saw us exiled from the U.N. Security Council, will all be blood on your hands tonight! For it is under your watch that you will let the millions who die of cancer every year continue to do so when it is proven that cannabis oil can save them! Tonight you will pay for the lives you took in the name of profit! In my hands I hold a vile of toxic radiation that, when vaporized, is potent enough to infect each and every one of you with the poison of cancer. Maybe *then* you will redefine your war on drugs."

Axel Benjamin rose up from his seat and slammed his fist on his table. "Are you nuts? This is terrorism! I thought you Hipsters were about political process? About the freedom to vote?"

"We *were* political," snarled the Hipster. "Before it got all mainstreamy. Now every idiot with an address can vote and an ignorant vote is worse than no vote at all! No…The only way to really see change is to make it yourself!

"You're insane!" Susan yelled.

The Hipster turned and met eyes with her and slowly walked over to her table. The room was so quiet you could hear the spurs on his boots clanking with every step. He stopped behind her and put his free hand on her shoulder. "Ah, the brilliant Dr. Drake–we meet again. Pity that such a mind must suffer the fate of these treasonous democrats…" He turned and glared at Axel Benjamin, "But the company you keep has sealed your tomb."

At that moment, a loud crash sounded off from above us and the moon roof smashed open. We were so busy watching the Hipster and his poisonous vile that no one had noticed the dark figure watching us from the roof. The intruder rained down with the shattered glass and landed hard on his feet in the middle of the dining hall. It was the Watchman, back from the dead and not looking too happy about seeing the Hipster's mitts on Susan.

"Get your hands off her," he growled.

"I thought I killed you..." The Hipster replied.

"You're not the only one with powers," said the Watchman.

"Well, let's see how many bullets you can take," smiled the Hipster. He signaled his gunman and they began to open fire. In seconds the Watchman had been hit multiple times, being pushed further and further back by the pressure of the bullets. He rolled over a table and out of sight.

The firing stopped. Gun smoke and the smell of gun powder filled the air. Some of the dinner guests started to moan and weep. The gunmen had to leave the Watchman alone to tell the dinner guests to shut up and sit still and I took that moment to sneak behind some press and slide behind the table where the Watchman was. He groaned in the midst of his rejuvenation.

I handed him the cuffs that Axel had given me. "Hang in there, buddy. We need you. Here take these..." I said. I demonstrated how to activate them by making an X with my wrists, "Just go like this and it'll activate a force field around your hands."

The Watchman did as I told him and when his wrists crossed each other both his hands lit up with a brilliant blue glowing orb of sonic waves that whistled and hummed with power. I'd never know because he covers his face, but I could swear he started smiling when those things activated.

"Thanks, kid." he said.

"I know Susan's your daughter," I said. "I know you're Stewart Drake."

The Watchman, who had been getting to his feet, stopped in his tracks. After a moment of thought he turned to me and said very plainly, "Tell her and I'll blow your dick off." Then he jumped over the table, back into battle.

I stayed behind the table stunned. *Blow my dick off?* I thought. *What a homo.*

But no, all jokes aside, he would literally detach my dick from my body if I told her.

The thugs began to open fire again, but this time it was different. The Watchman guarded his face and torso with the orbs whose sonic energy deflected the bullets while he charged at his assaulters one at a time using his new weapon to utterly destroy these motherfuckers. In a case where he would hit a gunman in the chest; their ribs would break and they would be sent flying through the air like a rag doll. In a case where the Watchman hit them in the face, they were not so lucky. Axel wasn't lying when he said those cuffs were good for blowing off heads. It was fucked up. Their heads exploded like water balloons.

Yeah, I took a couple pictures. The normal guy in me was scared as fuck, but the newsman in me kept poking his head up to snap some more pictures. By this time all of the gunmen were knocked out, paralyzed or decapitated. The only one left was the Hipster and you could tell he knew it. He grabbed Susan and got behind her, using her as protection.

"Let her go," the Watchman repeated.

"You of all people should share my ideals!" screamed the Hipster. "You take the law into your own hands because you believe the system is flawed, corrupted. The only difference is I am taking government into my own hands because I believe *that* system is flawed, corrupted."

"Please, just let me go," sobbed Susan.

I crept out from behind the table, spotting a gun one of the dead henchmen had dropped. I grabbed it and crept up behind The Hipster who was too focused on the Watchman to notice me.

"Hey, asshole," I said, pointing the gun to the back of his head. "Vote or die!" Then I pulled the trigger and with a loud **BANG!** I shot a bullet through the Hipsters head. It was the first time I ever shot someone in the head...or at all, I guess. He dropped to the floor, releasing Susan, who jumped back and saw me standing there with the smoking gun in my hand. The green vile of toxic radiation jingled as it rolled out of the Hipsters limp grip, along the floor and stopping at her feet.

She looked up to me. "Jake?"

"It's okay," I said. "He can't hurt you now. It's over..."

"You shot him...You saved me," she said in disbelief. By this point the dinner guests were racing out of the room and blue and red police lights flashed through the windows from outside. Susan and I stood still.

"Yeah, I'm probably going to jail for that..." I said. I looked around for the Watchman but he was nowhere to be found. I never even had the chance to thank him.

Susan didn't think I was out to get her after that night at the Pacific Rim. I mean, I shot a guy in the fucking head for her. If that doesn't say friendship I don't know what does. I was worried that I might be in a lot of trouble for that; sneaking in to a private event and shooting someone in the head, but when the cops got to the scene...The Hipster's body was gone...I suppose, in some way, the Hipster was victorious. The Conservatives lost and Stephen Harper was dethroned to make way for a new leader...Justin Trudeau of the Liberals. I hoped this change in government would satisfy the Hipster, wherever he was hiding. But if it doesn't, and the Hipster decides to attack once again, I'll be here...ready and willing to fight.

Story Three: The Freak That Washed Ashore

Where do I start? This story doesn't really have a beginning because the last story never really had an ending. They're sewn together like some sort of conjoined literary fetus, unable to exist without the other. So I guess the best place to start would be where we last left off, with me at the Conservative Party campaign wrap-up dinner, standing behind the Hipster with a gun in my hand, pulling the trigger, saving the girl and killing the bad guy.

Only I didn't kill the bad guy, did I? Despite putting a fucking *bullet* in his head, the Hipster got away. The powers he gained from injecting himself with Rejuvicell made a bullet wound to the head the equivalent of scraping your knee on the pavement. But despite his escape, we stopped the Hipsters plan to infect the Conservative Party leaders with a vile of toxic radiation.

Not only that, I got the exclusive eye witness account of the whole thing...and pictures to boot. The Sun ran the story on page one with a headline that read, "The Watchman Returns!" and below that was one of the pictures I managed to snap off while the Watchman was battling the Hipster's goons. Papers were flying off the shelves with people wanting to get a look at a real live superhero in their city. They never gave a fuck when he was out there saving homeless people but rescuing a politician like Georgio Mochella made him an overnight celebrity. And *I* became his spokesperson.

I was invited on several local news and talk programs, talk radio shows; I even got interviewed by Audrey Mason on Channel 5. And all of them asked the same questions, like, "Who was he?" "How did he get his powers?" and "What's the deal with those sonic blasters?"

Of course, I knew all the answers to those questions...but I wasn't about to reveal the Watchman's identity on live television. Not when Susan still didn't know. I couldn't tell them that the Watchman was really Dr.Stewart Drake, Susan's father, a pharmaceutical engineer for Axel Industries who was presumed to have died in a massive fire years before. Instead, I told them what they wanted to hear; cheesy shit that would sell more papers and ad spots. I said he never told me his true identity but based on his advanced technology and his super-human healing abilities, I assumed he had come from another planet and was here to protect the human race. And they ate it up.

They didn't know that his powers of healing really came from a serum he created called Rejuvicell. A serum he administered on himself in the midst of the fire to save his life–and make him the Watchman!

And they wouldn't ever know, because the Watchman swore to blow my dick off if Susan ever found out. He preferred that she continue to believe he was dead and remember him for the man he was, not the scarred "freak" he had become. But it is hard to keep a secret from the one you love. Especially one that you *know* would mean the world to her.

* * * * * * * * * * * * * * * *

"I wonder what he would think of this whole Watchman thing..." she said one night as we were out for dinner.

"Who?" I asked.

"My dad, silly."

When she said that, I nearly choked on my salmon.

"Why would you wonder something like that?" I asked.

"Well, he was a doctor and a very curious mind. He *discovered* Rejuvicell! The Watchman battled the Hipster, sure...but he was really fighting the Rejuvicell. I wonder what he would think about his creation being used for such evil purposes."

"I don't know," I said, hoping the topic would go away.

"Sorry I keep bringing him up," she said. "It's his birthday today."

I laughed, "It's the Watchman's birthday today?"

"No. My *dad's*. He would have been 43."

"Oh, of course," I said, covering my slip.

Just then my phone rang which, believe me, I was grateful for. Anything that got us off the topic of her father and the Watchman was okay with me. It was a private number, but I picked it up anyway. "Hello?"

"Hey, Jake," said the voice on the other end. "It's Jonah, the intern."

Jonah, the intern. Ever since that night at the Pacific Rim, he wouldn't leave me alone. He'd always find me in the office and let me know, in a joking way, that I stole the Hipster story from him. Because I took his press pass and sent him home. He was a ballsy little fuck...I might have respected him if he wasn't so awkward and annoying.

"Oh, hey Jonah," I sighed. "What's going on? I'm just on date night with the girlfriend...Why are you calling me from a private number?"

"You never answer when I call from my phone," he said.

That was true. He had me there.

"I'm a busy guy, Jonah. Can I help you with something or can I get back to my dinner? I have a *very* beautiful woman sitting across the table from me."

Susan brushed her blonde bangs out of her face and smiled.

"I was just calling to let you know that I'm not mad at you for stealing the Hipster story anymore," Jonah said, through the phone. "After tonight I'll have my own headline story and I'll be famous just like you. We'll be equals, you and I."

"What headline story?" I asked, pulling my eyes off Susan.

"Axel Industries is dumping drums of radiation waste from Fukushima into the pacific ocean."

He officially had my attention.

"Okay, you got me," I said. "Tell me more."

"I looked into their books and I saw high deposits from a toy company in Japan called ToTo Enterprise. It struck me as odd that Axel Industries would have a Japanese toy company on their client list...you know, reporter's instinct."

"So? What's your point?"

"So I looked into it further and ToTo Enterprise is owned by Eiji Zao, brother of Akira Zao—a head adviser on the Fukushima Nuclear Clean-Up committee. Akira has been paying Axel Industries to help dispose of nuclear waste from the 2011 meltdown and using ToTo Enterprise as a dummy company to launder the money."

"Can you prove any of this?"

"I have all my sources and documents on a USB Stick in my inside pocket," Jonah replied. "And after tonight I'll have video. I followed the dump trucks to the docks. They're starting to load the boats as we speak and I'm going to get it all on film."

Jonah was right. This was a huge fucking story. A big black cock of a story.

It was a chance to catch that son-of-a-bitch Axel Benjamin red handed and finally put him away for good, locked up in a cell with his old bodyguard Jeremy Stands, a.k.a. The Hooded Killer.

"Where are you right now?" I asked. I wrote the address he gave me on a napkin and hung up the phone.

"What was that all about?" asked Susan.

I signaled the waiter for the bill, "I gotta go."

"Go? What? Why?" she said as the waiter came over. I slapped a few twenties on his tray hurriedly.

"Big story," I said. "*Huge* story."

Susan was starting to get annoyed, "Can you please slow down and talk to me? What's going on, Jake?"

I dropped my napkin on my half eaten salmon and got up from my seat, "Axel Industries has been dumping nuclear waste from Fukushima off the shores of Vancouver."

She put her hand over her mouth, "Oh my god...Go. You have to go."

But I was already out of my seat and on my way.

****

I met Jonah at the docks at the address he had given me. I parked a few blocks down the road so as not to have my Civic spotted. When I got there I saw him fiddling with the zoom lens on his camera that he had attached to a small tripod facing three bright lights over the water in the distance. He smiled wide as he saw me approach. "Here," he said, tilting the camera in my direction, "Take a look."

I looked into the lens and saw the boats he was talking about. They were filled with oil drums, the last of which were being brought on by a dolly by some large men dressed in black. "And you're for sure that's nuclear waste in those drums?" I asked, tilting the camera back to him.

"How could it not be? The deposits from ToTo Enterprise, the relationship of the Zao brothers...All the pieces fit! It has to be nuclear waste!"

"Sssh!" I scolded, "Will you shut up? They'll hear us."

Then from behind me I heard a man say, "Too late."

Before I could blink, Jonah fell to the floor, knocked out from a blow to the head. I spun around to see one of the boatmen who had been loading the oil drums pointing a gun at me, showing his crooked teeth as he smiled. "You fucked up," he said.

"You took the words right out of my mouth," I told him.

From behind the gunman came a high pitched whistle, followed immediately by a deep rumble like that of a sub-woofer in a night club. Then, a flash of blinding light appeared and before my attacker could turn around to see what was going on, a powerful sonic beam from the Watchman's wrist blasters ripped him from where he stood and launched him over the railing twenty feet into the ocean as if he were a rag doll. I had seen those sonic blasters at work the night the Watchman took on the Hipster's goons and I was pretty certain that guy wasn't going to be swimming back to surface anytime soon.

"I saw you coming up behind him," I told the Watchman as he stood there in his shoulder-spiked leather jacket, his black bandanna blowing softly in the night breeze, "You're getting sloppy in your old age. Happy birthday, Stewie."

The Watchman switched off his orbs and the night became quiet once again. All that was heard were the waves softly crashing under us as the tide rolled in and out. "Don't call me that," he said. "Not if you're fond of your face."

In the distance I could see more boatmen running up the docks toward us, armed with guns. If they hadn't heard the sonic boom or the screams, they definitely saw the light show. Those sonic blasters lit up the sky like fucking fireworks. I pointed down the dock at them and said, "I don't think we're out of the woods yet!"

"What are we dealing with?" asked the Watchman.

"You don't wanna know," I said.

He turned his head to me, "Really? We've fought a Hooded Killer murdering the homeless and a Hipster who tried to give the Conservative Party cancer...How bad could this be?"

"Axel's dumping nuclear waste from Fukushima in our waters!"

The Watchman turned back to the oncoming boatmen. "Shit...That's bad. Take your friend and get out of here...I'll take care of these guys."

I didn't ask questions. I threw Jonah over my shoulder and took off up the dock as fast as I could. Behind me I could hear the chaos of sonic booms and bullets crackling. We made it back out onto the main street and I let Jonah off from my shoulder and laid him flat on the ground. I reached into the breast pocket of his jacket and pulled out the USB stick he had told me about on the phone.

I felt bad that I was about to swindle the kid out of another story, but I had to. Call it a personal vendetta, call it revenge, call it whatever—I had to be the one that brought down Axel Benjamin. I had to be the one who showed the world what kind of a monster he really was. Not for the fame or the money, but so that I could look him dead in the eye as they walked him into court and say, "I got you, you slick fuck!"

So I left Jonah there and I went back home to check the files. It took me about two hours of sifting through documents, account transfers and shit like that, but I got through it. There was enough to make a case but it wouldn't be a rock solid one. I was kicking myself in the ass for not grabbing Jonah's camera when I grabbed him. The video footage would have been a big help.

Then, as if some fairy godmother had heard my calls, there was a tapping on my window next to the fire escape. I jumped up from my seat and rushed over, expecting to see the Watchman...but he was nowhere to be seen. There, tied to the railing by the neck strap, in all its glory, was Jonah's camera.

****

The next day I got to the Sun Tower early to unload what I, or Jonah rather, had discovered to Mr. Dennis. Between the pictures, the account transfers and the relationship of the Zao brothers, I thought we had an air tight story. So when the Chief shut the story down without a thought, I lost it on him. "What do you mean you won't run it?" I yelled. "This story is *mega*. He's poisoning our shores with nuclear fallout!"

Mr. Dennis looked up from his desk, "When are you going to learn this, kid? There are powers greater than you and I at work here. I admire you running around with your 'save the world' hat on, high off your first big story and ready to get all Lois Lane, hero of the press sorta thing–but stop it, *right fucking now*, you understand? I'm warning you. If you keep knocking on the devils door, eventually someone is going to answer."

"People deserve to know!" I argued.

"Yeah, maybe they do, Jake," he said. "You don't think that I have had a thousand scientists, biologists, geologists and every other fucking "ologist" come into my office and sit where your sitting right now, telling me the same fucking thing that's coming out of your mouth this very moment?"

I threw my hands in the air, "So then why aren't you running this?"

Mr. Dennis sighed, rubbing his forehead, "Because, Jake," he said. " People may *deserve* to know, but people don't *want to* know. People don't want to know that the ocean life in the Pacific is coming to a screeching extinction. People don't want to know why they aren't allowed to swim in the ocean; they know it's bad but they don't want to know how bad. They don't want all the bloody details, they just want to stare at it on a sunny day and say, 'Aw, look at that. That's pretty.'

'People don't want to know about the things they can't see. They want to pretend everything is fine the way it is. Because if they *didn't*, that means they would have to change and let me tell you something about the human race, Jake—we don't like to change! And even if we did, *even if we did*, my bosses don't *want* things to change because if they did, *their* pockets would get a whole lot thinner. The world is a tragic mess, son. But not you, nor I, have the ammunition in our corner to do anything about it."

"Well, that's where you're wrong, Chief," I said. "I think we *do* have the ammunition!"

He threw his head back, "What? The Watchman? Your little super-hero buddy? Shit, kid, he sells papers, I will give you that. But he's just *one man*."

Tired of arguing, I put him to an ultimatum, "You either run this story, or I put it on the net."

"You will most definitely not!" he shouted as he slammed his fist down on his desk. "You are under contract with the Sun. You break your contract; you are out on the street!"

"I'll save you the trouble," I said. "I quit!" And then I slammed the door behind me as I walked out of his office.

At that moment Diana was just coming to her desk to start work. She smiled when she saw me...until she saw me.

"What happened?" she asked.

I told her what happened. She was baffled. At *me*.

"This is your job," she said. "Are you really going to throw everything away for a story? A story you're not even totally sure is true?"

"It's done," I said. "There's no going back."

She grabbed my wrist as I started to walk away, "Please, Jake. Don't do this…"

It was hard to do, walk away from Diana like that. She really meant a lot to me and, though she would never admit it publicly, I knew she had a soft spot for me too. But there were bigger things at work here than just me and D. I had to go.

I squeezed her hand and smiled, "Take care of yourself, okay? Stay out of trouble."

On my way out of the front lobby I bumped into Jonah on his way in. Luckily I had brought his camera with me that morning. I pulled it from my work bag and reached out to hand it to him. He ripped it from my hands, pointed his finger in my face and yelled, "Where's my USB stick?! *Where*?!" Then, to my surprise, he shoved me. That might have upset me if he wasn't so tiny, nerdy and cute.

I pulled the flash drive out of my pocket and handed it to him. "Mr. Dennis won't run it, I just came from there. It's a no-go, Jonah."

"I knew it!" he hollered, "You tried to steal my story…again! You've crossed the line this time, Jake!"

Between all that had just taken place, I didn't have much sympathy left for this kid. I had let him blow off some steam and even let him get away with a shove, but I had reached my quota. I pushed him aside and walked out to the street. He called out to me as I walked, "You'll pay, Jake Dunlop! Mark my words, I shall have my revenge!"

I could not believe this guy was *still* yelling. I put on my headphones and continued on my way. There wasn't a moment to waste. After all...I had an article to write.

****

When I got home I made myself a WordPress account and started putting things together. I had given Jonah back the USB stick with all the information exposing Axel Industries, but not before I made copies of everything on my home computer. By dinner time that evening the article was ready for print. I called the article, "Toxic Times by Jake Dunlop" and I shared it through my Facebook and Twitter accounts. I had recently gained over a hundred thousand followers after 'The Watchman Returns' article was published. I called them the Watchman Watchers. They were the guys who would share picture posts of sightings at #WatchTheWatchman, which usually just turned out to be blurry shots of some regular Joe Blow in a leather jacket. A few were legit though. And I would know if anyone. I was practically his agent.

111 | P a g e

I hit publish at 6:20 pm. By 9pm, I had broken the internet. The article had gone viral through the re-tweets of the Watchman Watchers, who triggered the liberal environmentalists, who seemed to really get on the "Fuck Axel" bandwagon with me. The article surfed its way around the net, even being shared by people who posted it to complain about how much other people were posting it. I didn't mind. Whatever their reasons, it was making noise.

The next morning, after a seemingly victorious night, Susan came over for an early lunch. We sat on my couch and I turned on my television. The 11 o'clock news with Audrey Mason was on and take a guess who she had on as her guest. Yup. Axel Benjamin. They smiled back and forth at each other as I listened to them crucify me on live TV.

"…It just really seems like a desperate act for attention," said Audrey. "So then, what were the money transfers from ToTo Enterprises for if not for an under-the-table kickback for dumping toxic waste in our waters?"

Axel smiled, "*Yes*. An "under-the-table" kick back that was completely on the books. These documents that were stolen from my possession are merely tax documents. My relationship with ToTo Enterprise and Eiji Zao has nothing to do with Akira Zao, nor the efforts to clean up the tragedy of Fukushima. Axel Industries produces a synthetic plastic for an action figure in Japan that is able to stretch and retract. It's a very popular item—Mr. Action, I believe his name is."

An image of a stretchy Mr. Action doll in its plastic casing appeared on screen. I felt a nervous feeling come over me. Was that possible? I never even investigated if he had any products being shipped...I didn't really investigate at all. I was so consumed with hatred for Axel that I went on entirely what Jonah had come up with. But...Jonah was a tool... What if he was wrong?

"If you're just joining us right now, we're talking about "Toxic Times", an article released on the internet last night by Jake Dunlop, who is most known locally for his sensationalist articles in the Sun about the Vancouver super-hero, the Watchman. Dunlop was recently let go from the Sun for undisclosed reasons. Editor, Paul Dennis has no comment on the matter but sources say that Dunlop had become angry and aggressive leading up to being fired from the publication. His article lashes out at Axel Industries, claiming they are responsible for dumping toxic waste off the Vancouver shores but carried no proof except vague transfer receipts and blurry photos. As his credibility diminishes, it seems this fly by night sensation may be nearing the end of his fifteen minutes..."

I clicked it off and tossed the remote aside. "*Wow*. I was not expecting that."

"That was a massacre," said Susan. "Even *I* kind of resent you right now."

I shook my head, "Even *I* kind of resent me right now...Is it possible I was so blinded with anger that I just assumed everything Jonah had prepared was true without fact checking?"

She put her arm around me and gave me a reassuring kiss on the cheek. "Be strong, babe," she said. "Your hearts in the right place...Fuck Audrey Mason."

I smiled, saying, "Yeah...fuck that bitch." Then I got up and started to bring our plates into the kitchen. In the kitchen I put the plates in the sink, turned on the tap and called back to her over the running water, "What will this mean for you at PharmCorp? Does Axel know you and I are dating? I'm not going to get you fired, am I?"

"I don't see why he would," she called back. "The most he could do is pull his funding. But that's not going to happen anytime soon. He's been pumping all kinds of money into new trial drugs since the incident with the Hipster at Pacific Rim. He's trying to recreate the Rejuvicell serum, I know it. I recognize the compounds in the data reports...."

Then she went quiet. She came back a moment later, saying, "Babe, your phone is vibrating! It's says 'Johnny-Cambie'...whose that?"

I turned off the tap and ran back into the room. I hadn't talked to Johnny in a while being that I hadn't felt the need to smoke weed since me and Susan started dating. But if he was calling, it probably was for good reason. He wasn't the type to call you just to say, "Hey, how's your day going?"

I took the phone out of Susan's palm and answered it, "Hey, Johnny. What's up? How's your day going?"

He was in a panic, "Jake! Fuck! Holy fuck! Jake! You gotta get down here! You gotta report this shit!"

"What's going on?" I asked.

"It's fucked!" he screamed. "Totally *fucked*! A monster just walked out of the water at English Bay, man! A big fucking green, fucking lizard monster, man! It's going after people! It's–It's killing them! Eating them! Get the fuck over here, man! Bring the Watchman! Stat!"

He was talking so fast, it was hard to understand him. "What?" I said. "Johnny, slow down I–"

But it was too late. Johnny had already hung up.

I leaped from the couch and went for my coat hanging on a chair in the kitchen. Susan swung her head around and yelled, "What was that? Where are you going?"

I told her as I threw on my coat, "*Apparently* there's a monster terrorizing English Bay right now...it killed some people. I have to go."

She raised her eyebrows in protest, "Are you crazy? There's a monster *killing people* at English Bay and *you* have to go? Did you just hear yourself?"

We didn't fight often, but when we did it was in the tone in which she was speaking

"It's my job, babe" I said, calmly trying to diffuse her.

She rebutted quickly with, "You *quit*, remember? It's not your job anymore."

I started for the door, "Okay then—fuck it! It's because those people need me! The Watchman will be there and I'm going to have his back whether you like it or not!" Then I left, shutting the door hard and loud so she knew I was finished arguing.

I walked down the hallway. By the time I got to the elevator, Susan was coming out of the apartment with her jacket half on and the set of keys I had given her in her hand. "Where are you going?" I asked.

She locked the door to the apartment and started towards me, throwing on the other side of her jacket. "I'm coming with you," she said.

I put up my hand, objecting. "No, it's too dangerous," I replied.

But it was no use trying to argue. "I'm coming *with you*," she said. "Get over it."

****

As we drove down Robson towards English Bay, we began to hear the screams of the men and women fleeing the beach strip. Before long they came into view, tearing down the sidewalks with a look of terror in their eyes that would make even the bravest of men think twice about where he was heading. I could see Susan was shook. I was too. We pulled up beside the laughing statues and that is when I first got a glimpse of the damage to the Bay. In the distance, a hundred or so feet out into the ocean, an oil tanker was slowly sinking beneath the surface. The muddy sand where the tide would roll in was dug out and thrown into mounds like someone had been digging for gold. By them, four dead bodies were tossed scattered on the beach; completely torn open around the stomach area...one of them was a little girl. I felt sick to my stomach. It was an utter massacre.

Then...I saw it. Well, no, not really. First I heard it. It made a deafening call, like a hawks caw, but toned lower like an elephant's trunk when it blows. That's the best way I can explain it but I can tell you this— it scared the shit out of everyone who was unlucky enough to hear it. Susan gasped and squeezed my hand. That's when I turned and saw it....

What a fucking Freak this thing was. It was something between a man and a lizard; walking upright on two feet but covered in a green, slimy, scaly exterior. A long tail swung behind the creature like a whip, and his yellow eyes, like that of a python, glared hungrily from left to right across the beach. The side of its mouth was stained a shade of rust from the blood of his victims and he was looking thirsty for more. Whenever the monster hissed, its gaping black hole of a mouth peeled back and showed off his fangs and fleshy gums.

I froze as he turned in our direction. It looked me right in the eye and hissed. Then it stomped his massive, three-toed flipper-foot into the dirt and lowered its head, preparing to charge.

At the same time, a high pitched squeal was rapidly getting louder behind me. Though I was too paralyzed with fear to move, I recognized the sound. It was a dirt bike and it was ripping closer *fast*! In seconds I watched the dirt bike blow by me with a thunderous roar, blowing dirt and sand behind it as it sped down English Bay. As I had somewhat suspected, it was the Watchman at the helm.

He drove with one hand on the throttle as the other hand lit up with a flash of light and fired a sonic blast that knocked the Freak off balance. When the creature got back to his feet it did *not* look happy. The monster charged towards the oncoming dirt bike like it was playing some sort of twisted game of chicken. The Watchman didn't change course, instead he accelerated and seconds before they crashed into each other the Watchman leaped from the bike, using the vehicle as a projectile. But this time, The Freak was ready. He swatted away the dirt bike and it flung to the side as if it were made of paper. I couldn't believe how strong this thing was. Even the Watchman looked stunned.

Susan grabbed me by the arm, pulling me out of my trance. "Come on!" she screamed. "Let's go!"

"I can't," I said. "I can't leave the Watchman."

"Why?!" she cried. "Why do you care so much about him?! I'm your girlfriend! He's a complete stranger!"

And that's when I said it. It just kind of slipped out. "He's your father, Susan!"

She let go of my arm and took a step back, "What are you talking about? What do you mean he's my father?"

As my attention split between Susan and the battle taking place behind me, I told her, "Your father didn't die in the fire at PharmCorp. He injected himself with the Rejuvicell just in time. It saved his life but the burns left him disfigured…He didn't want you to know because he wanted you to remember him how he *was*…not how he *is*…but that's him out there, Susan. The Watchman is your father."

She looked the other way and wiped the tears away from her eyes. Believe me, this wasn't how I wanted her to find out about it—but there was no more time for lies. At that very moment, on the sands of English Bay, the Watchman was losing the battle. His sonic blasts were doing damage when he could fire them off but the Freak was as agile as he was powerful and would slither out of the beams way just before they hit. On top of the monsters evasive defense, its massive claws would send the Watchman crashing to the ground each time they connected. Even with his powers of fast healing, he was getting cut bad and losing a lot of blood. Each time he fell, the longer it took for him to get back up. I could see he was exhausted. This wasn't like fighting the Hooded Killer or the Hipster—or any human at all for that matter. The Freak was twice his size, built like a brick wall and, most importantly, a fucking *man-lizard*!

Then I watched in horror as the Freak grabbed the Watchman and squeezed his head between its claws. His skull folded and bent like an aluminum can and he dropped to the ground...dead. Susan shrieked and looked away, sobbing.

I don't know why or what I was thinking but I started charging at the monster in a blind rage. Maybe I was too angry to think about death...or maybe death didn't matter. I lunged at the monster in an attempt to put my arm around his neck and choke the son-of-a-bitch. The monster swung his arm and it hit me like a tree log. Everything went black for a second and when I came to, moments later, the Freak was a good ten feet away from me and my face was bleeding pretty bad. He threw me like a pillow without blinking. My head throbbing, I felt Susan shaking at my arm.

"Wake up! Jake, wake up!" she cried, pulling harder. I got to my feet and we started running. I could barely see anything so I followed the sound of Susan's feet pounding against the asphalt and kept telling myself not to pass out. I couldn't give up now. The Watchman was dead...and we were all alone.

Story Four: In the Shadow of Heroes

"You have to turn me."

Susan paused from dabbing the blood around the bandage on my face, "What?"

"I need you to do what you did to the Hipster–to me," I said. "Inject me with the Rejuvicell."

"Are you crazy?" she asked. "For what?"

"You know for what," I said. "So I can fight this thing. So I can stop it. You *saw* what the Freak did to those people...to that child."

She shook her head vigorously, "No, no, definitely not. You're not going to go and get yourself killed. I lost my father twice. You're all I have. Can't we let the police handle it?"

She took a look in my eyes and immediately knew the answer. I think she knew it all along.

"Fine," she sighed. "Let's go."

****

As we drove we listened to the radio as the News about the Freak attacks went public, "The VPD and Animal Control are urging Vancouverites to stay in their houses after a large reptile attacked a group of families at English Bay only hours ago. The reptile is still on the loose and considered a life threatening danger to the public. Do not approach if seen. Among the dead today was the popular local vigilante, The Watchman, who was taken to the City Morgue along with the rest of the victims of this horrible tragedy..."

Susan turned off the radio as she parked in front of an old character house on Commercial Drive. She took the keys out of the ignition and nodded for me to follow.

"What's up?" I asked, confused at why we had stopped. "Aren't we going to PharmCorp?"

She chuckled, "Are you crazy? Axel Benjamin *wants* this serum. He has since the day he discovered my father was working on it. I'm not just going to leave the remaining samples of the stuff in a building *he has keys to*. This is a rental property my dad bought to help me pay for my school. But I haven't rented it out since he died...it doesn't feel right."

We walked up the yard and entered the house. Everything was old and creaky. The *door* creaked, the *floorboards* creaked, the *stairs* creaked...I felt like a strong gust of wind would have this house folding faster than a pair of deuces. Other than a few orphaned pieces of furniture, the house was deserted. I followed Susan up the staircase to an empty bedroom where she walked briskly over to a sliding door closet at the other end. She pushed the door aside and then pushed aside a hanger with an old maroon leather jacket paired with a red bandanna tied and hanging loosely off the collar. Dropping to her knees, she lifted up a false floorboard and pulled out a leather pouch. Inside the pouch were three syringes of a thin, golden liquid...Rejuvicell.

"You need to be injected with the right amount of adrenaline before taking the serum," said Susan. "Too little, the injection will stop your heart. Too much, it will *burst*."

I smiled nervously, "Well...That's comforting."

****

Back at the lab Susan prepped me for injection. I would be lying if I said I didn't have any second thoughts about what we were about to do. I trusted Susan and everything, but this wasn't piercing my ear or waxing my chest. An unbalanced combination of adrenaline and Rejuvicell would mean bye-bye Jake. And I wasn't the only one with doubts. Susan kept muttering, "You're such an idiot," over and over under her breath as she was connecting the vital readers. I didn't know if she was talking to me or herself. Before I knew it we were ready to go. She asked me one more time if I was sure I wanted to go through with this.

"Do it," I said.

She flicked a switched and I watched both the adrenaline and the Rejuvicell flow through the plastic tubes, into my body. In a second my muscles began to tighten and seize. I lost vision and blacked out...but when I opened my eyes, everything was different. Colors were brighter, smells were more distinct. I felt my biceps and forearms pulsing with strength like I could punch through a brick wall or lift up a car. I sat up in my chair and met eyes with Susan. She was in tears. "I...I thought I lost you," she said between weeps.

I put my hand to her face and wiped away her tears with my thumb. "I'm here," I said. "I'm good...I'm...*great*, actually."

I got out of my chair and danced around the lab. I was lighter, quicker and more agile than I had ever been before. I felt like I could swing dance for days at a time, that is, if I had any clue at all how to swing dance. Susan watched me and laughed. Then, suddenly her eyes went wide and she screamed, "Your cuts!"

She ran over to me and gently removed the bandage over the wounds I'd received from my short battle with The Freak at English Bay. She stepped back with such a look of shock that I thought she was disgusted but I touched my face and felt that the wounds had healed into nothing but scar tissue. I was starting to understand the power of what I was dealing with. I knew things were never going to be the same again.

"So what now?" asked Susan.

"The radio said they brought the Watchman to the City Morgue...Let's go get those blasters...It's time to pay Axel Banjamin a visit."

"You can't go like that," she said. She went back into the closet and pulled out the maroon leather jacket with the red bandanna tied around the collar.

I smiled. It was perfect. I put it on. It was snug, but it fit great. It was a real race bike jacket; it even had the metal plates in the elbow. I wrapped the bandanna around my face and tied it in the back. It tightened over the bridge of my nose and just under my eyes. I looked up to Susan and she took a step back.

"You're...You're just like him," she said.

I put my hand under her elbow and brought her close. I know it sounds gay but, because we both knew this might be a one way ticket to the graveyard, we just kind of stood there, holding each other for a bit.

"They *do* say girls end up falling in love with their father," I joked after a minute.

She bounced her head off my chest softly, "Shut up, shut up, shut up..."

* *

When we got to the City Morgue, it was closed for the night. "Come with me," said Susan, heading around the corner of the building.

I followed her to the back entrance where she dropped to her knees and pulled out a bobby pin from her hair. She then started to use the bobby pin to *pick the lock*! You have to understand what a mind-fuck that was. I had always pegged her so sweet and innocent but the more and more she showed herself, the more I *knew* she was the seed of the Watchman.

"Since when do you know how to pick locks?" I asked.

She giggled as she reminisced, "I went through a phase in high school. I had sex with girls and learned how to be a thief...rebelling against my "straight-edge" doctor father..."

"And you learned how to pick locks…" I repeated, still baffled.

She smiled, "Pick locks and eat box."

I felt my face getting hot, "Oh, really?" I said. "So you know all about that stuff then?"

"Oh yeah," she confirmed as she wiggled the bobby pin just right and the door clicked open. She opened the door and motioned me into the dark hallway like a geisha—but I wasn't finished talking.

"So…how do I do?" I asked, refusing to step forward until she answered.

She looked at me and smiled, pinching my cheek over the bandanna saying, "You're just *tops*. Come on, let's go."

Once the door was closed behind us we were engulfed in darkness. After a brief moment, the fluorescent lights started to flicker on and I saw Susan with her finger on the light switch, smiling. I'm not going to lie; it was starting to bug me that Susan was doing all the sneaky spy stuff. I mean, *I* was the guy with the bandanna over my face. She looked at me and laughed, knowing exactly what I was thinking.

"What?" she asked, fluttering her eyelashes and playing innocent, "I went to med school, I've spent a lot of time here. I know the layout."

"So I bet you know where they're keeping him," I said.

She started down the corridor. "Follow me," she said.

* *

The lights flickered over the body of the Watchman, stretched out on a medical table and covered in a thin white cloth from head to toe. The room was cold and smelled of sanitation. Susan and I stood over the body in silence, coming to terms once again that this time the Watchman was not getting up.

"It's weird," I said. "Standing over him like this...I can't believe he's gone."

"Just hurry," Susan said.

I didn't waste any time. One by one I removed the blasters from his wrists and put them on to mine. As the last bracelet clicked on, a headlight from outside shone through the mosaic window and beamed into the room causing both of us to turn our heads.

"Time to go," said Susan.

When we came out the back door there was a limo parked sideways in the middle of the lot. For a second I felt relieved, thinking it was just some aristocrat getting a back alley blowjob...but then *Axel Benjamin* stepped out from the vehicle and I knew things were about to get hairy. It would be foolish for me to assume that Axel would walk into a fight with me blind, with nothing up his sleeve. I knew him better than that. And it was the, "thing up his sleeve" that was making me nervous.

"What do you want?" I asked bluntly.

He grinned wide, like a human version of the Cheshire Cat. "Nice get up," he said. "I like the red."

"What do you want?" I repeated.

He put is finger to his chin, "Well, for *starters*, I would have to say, I'd like to know what my Head of Research is doing breaking into the City Morgue..." As he continued, a freight truck started to back into the alley, beeping as it reversed, Axel spoke over the noise, "But we all know the answer to that, don't we? The blasters look nice on you. They really bring the whole outfit together. We need to talk, Mr. Dunlop...You've been poking your nose around in business that does not concern you. Luckily for me, I found someone with a shared distaste for you, Jake. He came to me after you fucked him over, just like you fuck *everyone* over. Take your girlfriend for example, you've brought her into this and tonight she will pay for it with her life. You are poison, Jake. Everyone around you suffers...Well, no longer."

The back of the freight opened up and something inside, something heavy, started to move and shake the trucks exterior. I watched as a mechanical leg, a big one, stomped onto the concrete from out of the freight box. Then another leg hit the ground with a loud **BOOM!** A metallic exoskeleton about four times the size of a person emerged from the shadows of the freight box. Positioned inside the massive armor, his little dorky head sticking out of the top—was Jonah, the intern.

He glared at me and smiled, "I told you I would have my revenge, Jake!"

Scanning the mechanical suit, I could see the arms and legs worked on hydraulic pumps that Jonah must have controlled from the inside of the suit somehow. Wires poked out from the the knees and elbows and connected to some kind of control center on the back. The suit seemed to have its own set of sonic blasters as well which, I must admit, concerned me just a tad.

"100 tons of titanium alloy," boasted Axel, smiling at his asset. "Armed with an upgraded sonic blaster, flame thrower and rocket launcher. Meet…**The Juggernaut!**"

Jonah huffed behind him, "That can't be my name. Marvel already has a character called Juggernaut. He fights the X-Men."

"Oh," said Axel. "Well, then…" He recomposed himself and turned back to me, "Since this masterpiece will be the instrument of your death and the ender of your world, I invite you to meet…**Apocalypse!!**"

I laughed.

"Apocalypse is already a bad guy too," said Jonah, shaking his head.

"He even looks like Apocalypse," I added.

"No, he doesn't," said Axel.

"How would you know," I said. "You didn't even know who Apocalypse was. He totally looks like Apocalypse. He's got the blue chest plate, those shoulder pad thingies, and the silver metal arms…"

"He's right," said Jonah, his eyes glancing down at the suit. "We should think about re-painting."

Even Susan chimed in, "The resemblance is uncanny."

I chuckled, "X-men pun, very good."

"Silence! All of you!" yelled Axel, slamming his palm off the roof of the limousine. He turned to Jonah, "Kill them!"

The large machine stepped forward and Jonah raised his blasters. I turned to Susan, "Get out of here!"

"But–"

"Now!" I screamed.

She took off down the alley towards the street. Axel tried to go after her so, to stop him, I made an "X" with my wrists and the sonic blasters activated.   But not into the calm peaceful orb of light I had seen when the Watchman would activate them. Right off the bat they started firing wildly out of control, lighting up the back lot as beams crashed through the windows of Axel's limo, leaving the doors dented and crumpled like a discarded piece of tinfoil. Axel dropped to the ground and took cover behind a garbage disposal unit as Susan ran out into the street and out of sight.

"Unclench your fists, you idiot!" yelled Axel from behind the dumpster.

I relaxed my hands and the beams immediately retreated, leaving the ally quiet once more. First lesson in sonic blasting...Do *not* clench your fists. Not unless you're looking to seriously injure and/or kill somebody.

"My turn," said Jonah. He raised his right hand and clenched his fist. A stream of fire plumed towards me from his flame thrower, instantly engulfing me in the bright searing heat. The force of the blast sent me crashing against the wall of the morgue and I fell to the ground. Jonah laughed as I rolled around putting the flames out on my jeans and my bandanna. The pain was unlike anything I had ever felt before, but it only lasted a moment. As quick as it came, I could feel the Rejuvicell working its magic and new skin cells flooding over the old damaged ones seamlessly. It was incredible.

 I got to my feet, padding out the last of the flames. I wasn't hurt anymore, I was just pissed off.

"That's it, Jonah!" I screamed. "This ends tonight!"

He sprayed another line of flames in my direction but this time I took cover behind the front hood of the limo. When he finally stopped attacking to see where I was, I shot up from behind my hiding spot and fired two quick blasts, which connected, but didn't do a whole lot of damage to that titanium alloy. I ducked and ran alongside the length of the limousine, leaping out of the way just before a missile came whistling out of his arm, exploding upon detonation and sending the limo tumbling through the air. It crashed against the morgue's back entrance and erupted into a giant ball of flames that lit up the alley like the sun itself. It was clear Jonah wasn't fucking around. This guy was out for blood.

Directly above him, the iron platform to the buildings fire escape dangled on a broken hinge knocked loose from the explosion. His body may have been impenetrable but his little peanut head sure wasn't. It was completely exposed. "I can't wait to watch you die," he said, raising the arm with the missile launcher once again.

"Maybe you should sleep on it," I said. I clenched my fist and fired off a sonic bream just over his head that crashed into the fire escape, knocking the platform from its hinge and sending it falling hard on top of Jonah's crown. With Jonah knocked out, the armor suit tipped forward and collapsed. Titanium alloy clanked against the pavement and the night went quiet.

"No!" screamed Axel.

I turned and saw him curled up in the fetal position between the dumpster and the brick wall, watching in horror as his masterpiece lay powerless on the ground like a scrap car in a junk yard. Pieces of glass and broken limo crunched under my steel toe boots as I approached him. I disabled my blasters, crouched down and grabbed him by his silk tie.

"It's just you and me now," I said. I pulled him closer towards me and gave him a hard shake to let him know I wasn't fucking around. "What was in those barrels you were loading on the ships? If not toxic waste than *what*?!"

"*Bodies!*" he cried. "Are you satisfied? They were filled with bodies!"

I shook him again, "What do you mean *bodies*?"

"Test subjects," Axel replied, "Human trials. I was trying to recreate Rejuvicell! I have been ever since I discovered what it did to Drake. I knew what he was up to but I had *no idea* of the power the serum contained in its compounds...But there were mistakes in the math...there were complications..."

"What *complications*?" I growled, tightening my grip.

"Introducing a reptilian trait into human DNA is complex. In many of the subjects the reptilian DNA took over and turned them into…monsters."

He hung his head low trying to hide a look that I thought I would never get to see on the face of Axel Benjamin. It was a look of shame.

He continued on, "Of course, the genetic combination was too much for their bodies to handle and they all died."

Suddenly it all made sense. The Freak that washed ashore on English Bay was one of Axel's test subjects who crawled out of his drum, not a mutated fish monster caused by Fukushima.

"Do you realize what you've done?" I yelled, slamming my fist against the dumpster. "One of your test subjects is out there murdering innocent people! That Freak killed the Watchman!"

Axel grinned, "Yes, I suppose it wasn't all bad."

I was about to punch that piece of shit smile off his face when red and blue lights came squealing around the corner and two city squad cars screeched to a halt. Two officers quickly exited each vehicle and drew their pistols.

"Freeze, asshole!" said the Brut at the front. Their eyes panned over all of the destruction; the limo burning strong in the background, Axel's broken robot encasing a passed out Jonah and a mosaic of fire escape scattered throughout the Morgue's back lot. Then their eyes landed on me.

"Holy shit!" said the Brut's partner. "It's the Watchman!"

"How can that be the Watchman?" asked an officer who exited the other car. "He's dead!"

His partner chimed in, "He's got powers! Maybe he woke up!"

"He looks different," said the Brut at the front. "He's got no toque and that jacket ain't got no spikes."

From the floor Axel pointed to me, "Gentlemen, I can assure you this man, though his wardrobe has been slightly modified, *is* the fugitive known as the Hastings Watchman! Now *arrest him*!"

Just then the officers' walky-talkies started blowing up with a voice on the other end shouting frantically, "All units! All units! Proceed to Coal Harbor Marina! Officer down! Code...uhh...Code...What's the code for *big fucking lizard monster*?!"

The officers looked at each other with terror in their eyes. The Freak had surfaced once again and now more people were dying.

"Let me go," I said. "I can stop him."

"Don't let him go," Axel warned. "He's a *criminal*! Arrest him!"

The Brut at the front gave me a nod, "You ride with me, okay?"

Before I got into the passenger seat of the cruiser I turned to Axel and said, "This isn't finished."

He smiled, "I couldn't agree with you more."

****

The squad car screeched to a full stop at the end of Burrard Street. We got out and ran down the steps into Coal Harbor, following a trail of manic screams and gunfire. Running down the winding path I saw the Freak towering over the officers on the scene. A few of them were badly injured and the others were trying to dance around it, getting shots of when they could but the bullets had little effect on the monster. One by one the officers fell at the hand of the scaly predator. Some were lucky enough to get up...some were not.

"What's your plan?" asked the Brut, drawing his pistol and taking cover behind a bench.

I crossed my wrists and activated my blasters. This time I remembered to unclench my fists. "Win," I replied.

I left the officer's side and charged at the monster. As the VPD scattered, the Freaks vibrant yellow eyes centered in on me and the glow of the sonic orbs around my hand. It took a step back hissed violently.

I screamed, "Yeah, you remember these don't you, you ugly fucker!"

I fired off a blast that exploded against the monster's chest and knocked him to the ground. He slid and crashed into the iron bars of the sea wall. Then the Freak got to his feet and gave his head a shake before letting out one of those powerful 'caws' of his. The cops looked at me and then at each other. Everyone took a step back.

It charged towards me. Before I could get out of the way its long, reptilian tale came over its head and whip-slapped me in the side of the face, knocking me off balance. It was only for a second but a second was all it took for the monster to tilt its head like a chicken and take a peck at my arm.

And by 'peck' I mean 'bite', digging into my flesh with those sharp fucking fangs of his.

I screamed out into the night sky and fired off two quick blasts to put some space between us. The Freak stumbled back. I took cover behind a tree. In just a moment the searing pain cooled down, like an ice cube on a fresh, pulsing burn. I watched as, through the rip in my jacket, flesh and skin cells reproduced in front of my very eyes until the wound had completely vanished.

But even healed, I had no clue how the fuck I was going to stop this thing. I mean, the Watchman was a full-fledged super-hero. He dropped from buildings. He stole cars. He was a brilliant chemist. *I* had been in about three fights my entire life... what the fuck was *I* going to do? Fantasizing about going out there and kicking ass was a lot harder than *actually* going out there and kicking ass. But I took a deep breath and prepared myself for the next round anyway. Victory or not, I had made peace with the fact that I was going down swinging. Dead or alive, I was in it until the bitter end.

I stepped out from behind the tree and called to it, "All right, you mutant piece of shit! I'm done fucking around!"

I watched as its head slowly turned in my direction. When it saw me it huffed and snarled. It lowered its head and began to charge at me full speed. I lifted up my blasters to fire but before I could get one off another shot came from behind me and a section of flesh near the monsters right shoulder splashed open. The Freak shrieked into the night.

I turned around to see who had fired the shot and that's when I saw him; his sleeveless Guns n' Roses T-shirt, his brown corduroys and his snake skin boots—complete with actual spurs. He jerked back his head and let the night breeze carry his long, greasy hair over to one side of his face.

"The Hipster…" fell out of my mouth. I stood still, not sure of what to do. After all, I wasn't completely sure he wasn't going to shoot *me* next. To my surprise, he flashed me a smile and then raised his shotgun, returning aim on The Freak.

"I heard it all through my police scanner," said the Hipster. "I thought you might need a hand."

I was baffled. "*You*? Helping me?"

"We may have our differences," he replied. "But there is one thing we can agree on–this city is our home. And this asshole is not about to tear apart my home!"

I turned back to the monster as his yellow eyes flickered back and forth between the two of us.

Then, as if some imaginary bell went off in his slimy head, the Freak came back swinging.

I fired a blast, it dodged it. The Hipster fired a blast from the shotgun, it hit. The Freak howled. I fired another two blasts that connected this time and knocked the lizard on its back, falling onto the crumpled remains of the Marina office that sat like a pile of firewood, destroyed in the Freak's earlier altercation with the VPD. Back and forth we came at it with an onslaught of firepower. I shot. He shot. I shot. He shot. The boardwalk lit up like it was the fucking red carpet at the Oscars. Then, the pile of wood that was once the Marina office and the Freak who lay on top of it, dropped beneath the water's surface with a **KURPLUNK!**

We stood there, tensely waiting for the Freak to pop out of the water…but he never resurfaced. Finally, I turned off my blasters and reached out to shake the Hipster's hand. After all, I could have never defeated The Freak on my own. I, along with the rest of Vancouver, owed him a great deal of thanks. But he wanted no part of it.

"Save it," he said. "The next time we meet might be under a less-inviting circumstance. No point in muddying things up with feelings."

I scratched my head, "You certainly are an onion. Many layers."

"Speaking of layers," said the Hipster, turning and walking away, his spurs clanking softly. "It's time that I returned to mine."

And with that, he was off. Behind me I heard the heavy paddle of footsteps approaching. Out of breath, the Brut I had rode in with took of his police cap and wiped the sweat off his brow with his forearm saying, "Geeze, I've never seen anything like that in my entire life! What do you suppose that was?"

"That was a monster," I said. "And there are more of them out there..."

The Brut looked over to his squad and then back at me. "Well, you better get out of here," he said. "The word is to arrest the vigilante known as "The Watchman" on site but...I'm not going to be the guy dumb enough to try it."

"Thanks," I said.

"No," he replied. "Thank *you*."

I took off down the path of the seawall just as more sirens and press vans started to arrive on the scene. I wondered what would the story be in the morning paper? That used to be something I cared about. That used to be a question for Jake Dunlop.

But Jake Dunlop's story had come to its end. And The Watchman's story was just beginning...

The End

Gregory Patrick Travers is a Canadian author whose works include the novel "Bald Guys: The Greatest Conspiracy Never Told" and the short story collection "Butt-Clenching Tales of Action & Adventure"
He also runs a short story website www.roundfirelegends.net that publishes a new short story every month.

Look up RoundFire Legends on Facebook.
Follow @gregorytravers on Instagram.
Follow @gregory_travers on Twitter
ALL BOOKS AVAILABLE ON
roundfirelegends.net
Createspace.com
Amazon.com
ASK YOUR LOCAL LIBRARY TO ORDER

Made in the USA
Columbia, SC
17 April 2018